D1157033

Scottish
Bakehouse
Mysteries™

Settling Auld Scores

Sandra Orchard

Annie's®
AnniesFiction.com

Books in the Scottish Bakehouse Mysteries series

. . . and more to come!

Library of Congress-in-Publication Data
Settling Auld Scores / by Sandra Orchard
p. cm.
I. Title
                    2021937177

AnniesFiction.com
(800) 282-6643
Scottish Bakehouse Mysteries™
Series Creator: Shari Lohner
Series Editor: Elizabeth Morrissey
Cover Illustrator: Kelley McMorris

10 11 12 13 14 | Printed in South Korea | 9 8 7 6 5 4 3 2 1

1

Laura Donovan scanned the high school football field from the hearse's front seat. She wasn't on her way to a funeral, merely riding in the passenger seat of the old LaSalle used by her Scottish bakehouse, Bread on Arrival, as a delivery van. She generally disliked the hearse, though she knew that the eye-catching vehicle did a lot to promote the business she co-owned with her best friends, Molly Ferris and Carol MacCallan, when it was being driven around their adopted town of Loch Mallaig, Michigan.

Since it had been marketing wiz Molly's idea to repurpose the hearse when they'd bought the former funeral home that housed their bakehouse, she had no qualms about driving it. "Do you see Henry?" Molly asked while scanning the lot for a parking space.

Laura shook her head. "The players aren't warming up on the field yet. It's probably just as well his teammates don't spot his aunt arriving to watch the game in a hearse."

"He's been living with you for two months," Molly said. "I think they know who you are by now."

Laura glanced at the field again and bit her lip. "Is it weird that I'm nervous?"

"Weird that you, Laura Donovan, former Manhattan master chef, are nervous? Maybe." Molly shrugged. "But tonight's qualifier game is the first step in getting to the state championship. It's a big deal for Henry and the others. And parenting, even in the short term, will bring out emotions you never realized you could feel."

"You'd certainly know."

Molly chuckled. "My nerves don't get quite the same workout as they used to now that Chloe is an adult and living in Milwaukee." She braked after a second unsuccessful pass through the parking lot. "I'll let you out here, then catch up with you after I park down the street."

"I can walk from wherever you park," Laura protested.

"Not with all the bakery boxes of goodies you brought for the tailgating party. Good thing Fergus got here early enough to stake out a place for us." Molly pointed to Fergus MacGregor's chrome Range Rover six parking spaces from the entrance to the field, her face beaming. Now that she was actually dating the man she'd crushed on when she'd been no older than Laura's nephew, the smile seemed to be a permanent fixture whenever he was around. Molly's hand stole to the bangs of her blonde bob, as if to ensure every hair was still in place. "He's already got his grills heating and chairs set up in the grass."

"Perfect." Laura clambered out. The cool November air bit at Laura's cheeks, and she pulled up her hood before grabbing a couple of bakery boxes out of the back of the LaSalle.

"Leave the tote with the napkins, plates, and face paint," Molly called back to her. "I can bring those."

College-age bakehouse employee Bridget Ross trotted over from the crowd of tailgaters. "Here, Laura. Let me help you."

Laura grinned. "How are you always right where I need you, Bridget?"

Bridget chuckled. "It's a gift." The breeze ruffled her long, black hair, which she'd streaked with green and gold for Loch Mallaig High's school colors.

Once she and Bridget had their arms full, Laura pushed the door closed with her hip and took in the excited crowd. "I feel so out of my element," she admitted to the younger woman as Molly drove away.

"This is only the second of Henry's games I've attended, and I haven't been to a tailgate party since college."

"High school tailgates are way tamer and, in my opinion, tons more fun because they're family oriented." Bridget nodded toward a grassy space adjacent to the parking lot. "Look, they've even set up games for the younger children. I brought supplies for making balloon animals, and Molly will do face painting."

The butterflies in Laura's stomach started to mellow as they headed toward Fergus's SUV. "Back in the Stone Age, when I went to high school, we never did anything like this. And living in NYC for the past couple of decades, I've missed out on opportunities to cheer on my niece and nephew."

"I think it's great that you were willing to take Henry in while his mom and dad are on their mission trip to South America."

"I'm happy I could help," Laura said. "His sister, Adina, is in her first year of college back in Marquette. She's living on campus and far too busy to take responsibility for her brother. Henry balked at leaving the country because he wants to be seen by college football scouts this season."

"If he's planning on playing college ball, then he made the right choice," Bridget said. "He's a great kid."

Laura grinned. "I think so, but I could be biased. I appreciate your making time to help him."

"My pleasure." Bridget, now in her final year of college, had been tutoring Henry in a couple of subjects in which his school transfer had left him a little behind. A decent grade point average was important if he didn't want to lose his spot on the football team.

"Hello, ladies." Fergus relieved Laura of her bakery boxes and set them in the back of his open Range Rover, then took Bridget's. "Where's Molly?"

Laura suppressed a chuckle, unsurprised that his first question was about Molly. "Parking down the block."

He nodded. "It's a great turnout. Carol and Harvey and their grandkids are around here somewhere. Moving a little slower with the twins in tow."

"What about Jenny?" Laura scanned the crowd for the MacCallans' daughter, who taught chemistry at the high school.

"She's on concessions duty," Fergus said. He paused, eyes twinkling, before adding, "Is Trent coming?"

At the mention of the relative newcomer to Loch Mallaig, Laura nearly blushed. She wasn't prone to girlish giddiness when romance was concerned, but something about handsome, adventurous Trent McKade brought out her inner teen. "I'm afraid not," she answered. "He had a group come into Northern Woods Outfitters yesterday asking for advice about an overnight backpacking trip. One thing led to another, and he wound up offering to serve as their guide. He'll be back tomorrow night."

"Sounds like Trent," Fergus said with a chuckle.

"Is Neil coming, Fergus?" Bridget asked, her casual tone sounding slightly forced to Laura's ear. Bridget and Fergus's son, who was in his midtwenties and served as Fergus's right-hand man at the family-owned Castleglen golf resort and lodge, were casual acquaintances as far as Laura knew—but could there be more to the relationship? She shook her head, not wanting to give in to the same sort of speculation that she disliked when it was done about her own romantic pursuits.

"I'm afraid not, Bridget," Fergus answered. "He's coordinating a formal dinner at the resort tonight." When her shoulders slumped slightly, he added, "But I'll be sure to let him know you asked about him."

"Here we are," Carol announced, arriving at the Range Rover holding one grandchild's hand in each of hers. Seven-year-old twins Maisie and Gavin sported matching hints of rosiness in their cheeks.

"It's our first game, Miss Laura!" Maisie crowed.

"I'm certain it will be very special then," Laura said.

Behind them, Harvey tugged a giant cooler on wheels. "If you're thirsty, we brought soft drinks, juice boxes, and water." He held up the grocery sack in his other hand and grinned at Laura. "And lots of candy because I know your nephew is going to deliver us a pile of touchdowns."

Jumping up and down, Maisie and Gavin let go of their grandmother's hands and cheered. Laura chuckled. Until last week's game, she hadn't been familiar with the local tradition of tossing candy to the children after a touchdown.

Harvey inhaled appreciatively as he wheeled the cooler over to where Fergus had set up a pair of charcoal grills on the asphalt beside his car. "The smell of fresh coals has me missing summer."

Fergus glanced at his watch. "I guess I'd better get our meal going too." He unlatched a cooler with the logo of the King's Heid Pub on it, the restaurant he owned as part of Castleglen. "I brought hamburgers, sausages, and hot dogs."

"Sounds yummy," Bridget said as she tied off the end of the long balloon she'd filled. She quickly fashioned it into a poodle for Maisie.

"Can you do a dinosaur for me?" Gavin begged.

"Of course," Bridget said, then raised an eyebrow. "But you forgot the secret word."

Gavin frowned in thought for a moment, then his eyes lit up. "Please!"

When Bridget handed him his requested dinosaur, a swarm of children surrounded her to make requests.

Molly joined the group, sneaking around the boisterous children to greet Fergus with a sideways hug. "Have you seen Henry yet?" she asked Laura.

Laura's dozing butterflies erupted into a fresh frenzy. "No. Do you think the coach will let the players join the pregame party?"

"I don't see why not," Molly said. "They don't need to get dressed and onto the field for warm-ups for a while yet."

"It depends on how focused Coach Bassett wants them to be," Fergus chimed in. "Loch Mallaig High's football team has never made it to the state finals, but this year lots of people think they have a real shot at it."

Laura wrung her hands. "First they have to win today's game, then get through next weekend's tournament, then the one after that—"

Carol clasped her warm hands around Laura's. "Just enjoy today."

Laura nodded. "You're right, of course. It's just that I really want Henry to do well. He said there will be college scouts at the district finals next week. And he absolutely lights up when he talks about playing college ball."

"Does he want to play for Michigan State?" Fergus asked.

Laura laughed. "I think he's hoping for Alabama or Florida. Someplace a little warmer."

"Smart boy." Harvey blew on his cupped hands to keep them warm.

Fergus shook his head. "Too much time in the sun will make him soft."

"Who are you calling soft, Mr. MacGregor?" Henry appeared from between two cars, his bright eyes twinkling. His blond hair gleamed in the sunlight, and he wore a team jacket. Laura blinked, wondering if he'd grown yet again since that morning. He seemed to shoot up inches at a time without her noticing. Now well over six feet tall, he towered over his aunt.

"Not you." Fergus clapped the boy on the shoulder. "Good luck out there today."

Henry ducked his head. "Thanks."

Harvey cleared his throat. "I heard Marcus Parish is coaching your opponents today. Does that have Coach Bassett worried?"

Henry shrugged. "Not that he's said."

"Who's Marcus Parish?" Laura asked.

"Loch Mallaig High's former football coach," Fergus explained. "The principal fired him before the end of last season for failing to appropriately supervise his athletes at an away game."

"Why would his coaching the opposing team worry our new coach?" Molly asked.

"Karl Bassett was Parish's assistant last year, so unless Bassett really changed things up, Parish likely knows the man's playbook inside and out."

"Don't worry," Henry assured them. "We've got moves the Marauders won't see coming."

Henry hung around long enough to down a hamburger, a sausage, and half a dozen Empire biscuits, then headed to the locker room as the bakehouse's other part-time helper, Hamish Bruce, arrived. A retired history teacher, the tall, white-bearded handyman had a knack for oversharing trivia and a curmudgeonly demeanor, but the Bakehouse Three loved him all the same.

"Ooh, a birdie." Maisie pointed past Hamish to a man-size duck strolling through the parking lot, occasionally flapping its giant, black-and-white wings.

"That's Larry the Loon, our team's mascot," Carol explained.

"Like the birds we hear calling across the lake?" Gavin asked.

"That's correct, young man," replied Hamish, an avid bird-watcher. He gestured to the emblem on the retro green-and-gold jacket he wore, which likely heralded from his teaching days.

"Why is he here?" Maisie wanted to know.

"The mascot helps get the crowd excited to cheer on the players," Bridget said.

The young man wearing the costume must have noticed Maisie's fascination with him because he came over and crouched so he was at eye level with her. "Are you loony for the Loch Mallaig Loons?"

Maisie giggled. "I want them to win."

"That's good." The bird high-fived her. "Cheer good and loud." He offered her a team button and her eyes widened with awe.

"Can I keep it?" she asked Carol.

"Of course," replied her grandmother. "I'll help you put it on."

After handing over a pin for Gavin as well, the mascot moved on to the next family. Their pins secure, Maisie and Gavin ran to join a dark-haired teenage girl who had been walking with the mascot and was now showing another group of kids how to make maple keys, the winged seeds from maple trees, fly like helicopters.

Before long, volunteers roamed through the parking lot asking the tailgaters to start cleaning up as the game would soon start. Molly broke open a box of garbage bags she'd brought for the job and they all pitched in. Carol collected the twins, and the group headed to the side of the stands reserved for the home team. On the other side, their opponent's fans had a respectable showing. Laura and her friends claimed seats on the fifty-yard line, the benefit of arriving early with the tailgaters.

A few minutes before the game started, Hamish's cheerful wife, Joyce, and their four granddaughters joined the little group. Although the youngest, two-year-old Janine, stayed with Joyce, the older three girls, ranging in age from five to ten, joined Maisie and Gavin. Noticing the team logos that Molly had drawn on the twins' faces, Courtney, Alannah, and Leah begged for their own, and Molly happily complied.

The first quarter passed uneventfully, although Laura found it difficult to ignore the pair of teenage spectators berating the Loch Mallaig players' performance from just outside the fence ringing the field. From their belligerent attitude and leather jackets, they seemed as if they would be more at home in a motorcycle gang than at a sporting match, and Laura couldn't help wishing they'd stop poisoning the atmosphere for everyone else and leave.

"When's the candy toss?" Maisie asked impatiently.

"When they score a touchdown, duh," her brother said.

Carol scowled. "Please watch your tone, Gavin."

Maisie frowned. "Well, when are they gonna score a touchdown?"

Hamish's granddaughters chimed in with similar grousing, clearly growing equally bored.

"You never know," Fergus said brightly. "They could surprise you when you least expect it."

Hamish shook his head as one of their players fumbled the first pass of the second quarter. "*Och,*" he groused in the Scottish brogue commonly heard among locals. Loch Mallaig had been founded in the early 1800s by Scottish pioneers, and the town held their heritage in high esteem. "The whole lot of them seem to be off the fang."

"What's that mean?" Laura asked. She had picked up quite a few Scottish expressions in the time she'd been here, but this was a new one to her.

"Not up to their usual skill or power level," Fergus translated.

"They're awfully squirmy," Bridget observed.

Molly cocked her head, her gaze fixed on the players. "I was thinking the same thing. And they're itching themselves like crazy. Did you notice?"

Laura studied Henry. She'd been so focused on willing him to score a goal that she hadn't registered the way he kept running his fingers around the collar of his jersey and scratching the back of his neck, his arms, anywhere he could reach. She sank her teeth into her bottom lip. "I bought a different brand of laundry detergent last week. You don't think he's having an allergic reaction to it, do you?"

"Not unless you did the whole team's laundry," Harvey said. "They're all acting weird."

The opposing team intercepted the ball and pressed toward the end zone. Loch Mallaig's left tackle barely managed to take down the opponent's linebacker at the ten-yard line.

Larry the Loon jumped in front of the grandstand and urged fans to cheer on their team. Loch Mallaig managed to block their opponents and hold the score at zero until halftime.

Laura rose. "I'm going to talk to Henry and find out what's going on."

"I'll come too," Bridget volunteered.

By the time Laura and Bridget wound their way from the stands into the school, the team had already disappeared into the locker room. Laura spotted the team's redheaded equipment manager hovering in the hallway outside the locker room door and thought he was acting unusually nervous—biting his lip, rocking from one foot to the other, glancing around the slightly open door every few seconds—so she nudged Bridget and said, "Let's see what he knows."

The young man grimaced when Laura and Bridget stopped in front of him.

"What's going on?" Laura asked as they approached. "My nephew is on the team, and he and the other players seemed pretty itchy out there."

The teen's head bobbed affirmatively, but he said nothing.

Coach Bassett stormed out of the locker room, his ample height, barrel chest, and dark, slicked-back hair adding to his intimidation factor. "Brendan!" he bellowed at the now cowering teen. "Tell me right now—how did itching powder get inside the entire team's shoulder pads?"

2

Brendan's face was white as a sheet. "I, uh . . ." he stuttered.

"Speak up," Coach Bassett demanded. "You're in charge of the equipment. It's your responsibility to ensure no one tampers with it."

The boy attempted to stand taller. "I cleaned all the pads and hung them back in place after the last game, but anyone could've gotten to them between then and now."

"You should have checked the equipment before the boys dressed today," the coach barked.

A petite blonde strode up to them, hands fisted. "Aren't you being a little too hard on Brendan?"

"I can take care of myself, Tina," Brendan hissed under his breath.

"Don't let them push you around." Tina glared at Coach Bassett. "It's not as if anything like this has ever happened before. It wouldn't occur to *anyone* to scrutinize the inside of the shoulder pads for powder residue. Besides, if anyone should have noticed, it's the players when they put them on."

Coach Bassett gazed coldly at the girl for a moment, but her logic was sound. With an aggrieved sigh, he addressed Brendan. "The boys hit the showers to try to scrub the stuff off. They can wear their practice pads for the second half of the game. You break out the new jerseys, then clean every scrap of equipment they wore today."

"The jerseys are in the supply closet," Brendan stammered, gesturing to a door down the hall.

"Then you'd better get them out of there," Bassett said impatiently, tossing him a set of keys.

Brendan scurried down the hallway without glancing at Tina. She gave the coach one last spiteful glare, then spun on her heel and left the way she'd come.

A teacher passing them in the hall muttered to the student beside him, "Those would be the jerseys that cost the track team a new pole vault pit."

"Are you behind this, Coach Nelson?" Coach Bassett shouted after the teacher.

Coach Nelson spun around. "Behind what?"

"The itching powder in my boys' jerseys."

Nelson chuckled. "Is that why they looked so pathetic? No, I wouldn't pull a prank like that for such an important game. I may not like that you've managed to hijack the entire athletic department's budget, but I wouldn't jeopardize our school's chance at going to State over it."

Coach Bassett's single nod indicated he believed him, and Nelson and the student moved on. Bassett peered skeptically at Laura. "May I help you?" he asked, his tone clipped.

"I'm Laura Donovan, Henry Donovan's aunt. I came in to find out what was wrong and if there's anything I can do."

Bassett snorted derisively. "Pray the showers get rid of the itch." He strode to the locker room and pushed through the door.

Laura and Bridget started back out to the field. Before they got to the door, the mascot burst through it in a flurry of faux feathers.

"Is the team coming?" the loon asked Brendan, who was approaching the locker room with a cardboard box in his arms that must have held the new jerseys. "Halftime is almost over."

Brendan filled in the mascot on what had happened.

The mascot removed his headgear and chuckled, his bright blue eyes dancing with amusement. "That'll teach the guys to think twice before picking on you."

"I didn't do it, Kit!" Brendan insisted. "You know I wouldn't."

"Sure." Kit shrugged. "But the point is you *could* have, and that's a power over them those guys need to know about if you want to get any respect from them."

Brendan frowned, then mumbled something about the team jerseys and disappeared into the locker room. The mascot replaced his costume's headgear and trotted past Bridget and Laura toward the door. He burst through it and released a birdcall, earning a few answering cheers from the fans mingling on the path.

"Poor Brendan," Laura said as she and Bridget followed Kit through the doorway. "It sounds like he's being bullied."

Bridget nodded. "In my experience, football players have a bad habit of exploiting their big-man-on-campus persona by picking on the school's geeks." When Laura frowned, Bridget added, "Don't worry. I don't think Henry's like that."

"I'm glad to hear it." Laura checked the countdown clock on the scoreboard. "We'd better get to our seats. The second half is about to start." Granted, it couldn't start until the team was dressed, but she hoped that wouldn't take long.

Fortunately, when they returned to their seats, both teams were marching back onto the field and play began shortly. Once settled on the bleachers, Bridget and Laura filled their friends in on what had happened.

"Who do you suppose was behind the prank?" Carol asked.

"One of their opponents, I imagine," Laura said.

The fans surged to their feet with a deafening roar as Henry, the Loons' running back, broke through their opponent's defensive line. A player took him down five yards from the end zone.

Laura shuddered, but did her best to not betray her anxiety over the hit.

With thumb and finger to his lips, Fergus let out an ear-piercing whistle, then joined the clapping. "Seems as if the team's anger over the prank has ignited something in them."

"Like rocket fuel," Harvey agreed.

"About time," Joyce groused. For such an affable woman, she took her high school sports very seriously—often to the amusement of her friends and family.

Maisie jumped up and down. "Do we get to catch the candy now?"

The other children's eyes lit up at the question.

Laura chuckled. "If they can get the ball another few yards."

On the next play, the quarterback feigned a pass to one player then spun and snapped the ball to Henry in the end zone for a completion. The crowd leaped to their feet, bellowing with excitement.

"Now?" Maisie shouted.

"Now," Carol said, and all the children in the stands dashed to the front of the bleachers as fans tossed them candy. The kids caught most, then scrambled after the ones that fell to the ground. Unfortunately, Gavin came up empty-handed and appeared close to tears.

Larry the Loon must have noticed, because he scooped up some from the ground below the stands and handed them to the dejected little boy. Gavin dashed back to his grandma and proudly displayed what the mascot had shared with him.

"They chose a real sweetheart to be their mascot," Molly said.

The children settled back in their seats to enjoy their candy and await the next touchdown. And the Loons did not disappoint. By the end of the game, they'd racked up three touchdowns and trounced the Marauders twenty-one to three.

As the rival teams shook hands, Laura hurried to the field to congratulate her nephew.

Henry's grin lit his whole face. "We did it!"

"You certainly did." Laura beamed. "I'm so proud of you."

"Is it okay if I go out with the guys to celebrate?" Henry asked.

"Of course," Laura said. "Just make sure you're home before midnight. We have church in the morning."

As she watched Henry run off to catch up with his buddies, Laura spotted Karl Bassett having a heated exchange with the Marauders' coach.

"I know you were behind that prank, Parish." Coach Bassett's deep voice carried across the distance to where Laura stood. "If you try anything else like that, I'll make sure you never work in football again."

"I had nothing to do with it," Parish shot back. "But I wouldn't expect you to believe me. Clearly you haven't changed. Your false accusations already got me fired from one job—a job you neatly took over, I see."

"And I'm doing it far better than you did." Bassett jerked a thumb toward the scoreboard. "As you can see."

Not interested in hearing more from the feuding coaches, Laura left the field. She caught up to Molly and Fergus in the parking lot, where they were talking and laughing beside his Range Rover. "Sorry, Molly. I didn't mean to keep you."

"It's no problem," Molly said.

"Laura, we were talking about getting dessert at King's Heid Pub," Fergus said. "Would you like to join us?"

Laura knew better than to intrude on the lovebirds' date. "Thanks for the invitation, but I think I'll pass. Although I'm sure it'll be delicious."

Fergus chuckled. "Considering you make our desserts, I'm sure you're right."

"I'm ready when you are, Fergus." Molly grimaced slightly. "Laura, do you mind driving the LaSalle back to the bakehouse? It's parked down the block."

Laura wrinkled her nose dramatically, then laughed. "Fine, but I wouldn't do it for anyone else."

Laura got the keys from Molly and saw the pair off. As she was starting down the sidewalk, her phone dinged with an incoming text message. She checked the screen and was surprised to see that Bridget had texted her. *Come to the boys' locker room.*

Laura considered asking for an explanation, but she decided instead to just do as Bridget had asked. Inside the school, the halls were deserted, all students and athletes having cleared out in record time. Laura found the boys' locker room and knocked on the door.

No answer.

She nudged it open. "Hello?"

"Over here," Bridget's voice came from inside.

Laura's heart hiccuped as she glanced both directions down the hall to ensure nobody saw her. Seeing no one, she ducked inside. The door clanged shut behind her and she jumped. If the custodian locked the locker room door before he left, they'd be trapped inside for the rest of the weekend. She studied the narrow windows that edged the top of one wall. She might be able to wriggle through one, but how would they get up there? She shed her jacket, wadded it into a ball, and propped the door ajar.

"What are you doing?" Bridget asked as she joined Laura.

"Ensuring we don't get locked in here. What are *you* doing?"

Bridget held up a couple of small plastic bags, her eyes bright. A white powder coated the inside of each bag. "I got to thinking that if I could figure out what the itching powder is made from, I might be able to determine where it came from and who bought or made it." She jiggled the bags. "I managed to scrape these samples off a couple of the benches and the floor. Lucky I had these in my bag."

"That forensic science major sure is coming in handy, isn't it?"

Bridget grinned. "Exactly. You know the police won't investigate what seems like a high school prank, but I'm not sure that's all it was."

"Coach Bassett would agree with you." Laura picked up a crumpled piece of paper and started toward the trash can. "I overheard him—"

"Wait," Bridget interrupted. "Let me see that. It could be a clue."

Laura assessed the narrow yellow sheet. "It's a carbon copy of a parking ticket."

"Whose?"

Laura squinted at the smudged information. "I can't tell. I can only make out a couple of numbers in the license plate. It's dated days ago for parking in front of a fire hydrant on Balmoral Lane."

"Must be the one by the library." Bridget took the paper from Laura. "I'll hang on to it. Might prove someone was in here who shouldn't have been."

"Good point," Laura agreed.

"Now, what did you overhear the coach say?" Bridget prompted as she tucked the ticket into another plastic bag.

"Coach Bassett accused Marcus Parish of covering the uniforms with the itching powder, no doubt to ensure his team won the game and maybe as payback for Loch Mallaig High firing him."

"What did Coach Parish say?"

"He denied having anything to do with it, naturally."

Bridget stuffed the bags into her jacket pocket and resumed scrutinizing the benches. "In one of my tutoring sessions with Henry, he mentioned that the Loons' quarterback, Jason Johnson, was assaulted on his way home after a game."

"He never told me about that." Laura's heart thumped, worrying that something similar could happen to Henry. Was this how a mom felt when she sensed that her child was in danger?

"He probably didn't want to upset you. Jason wasn't seriously hurt, but Henry said he could've been if Henry hadn't happened by when he did."

"And you think the two incidents might be connected?"

Bridget shrugged. "This year's Loons have a real shot at making it to the state championship. For all we know, this could be part of a systematic attempt to undermine the team and keep them from getting there."

Laura frowned. "You really think so? An assault is a lot more serious than a summer-camp itching powder prank."

"You saw some of the parents out there. People take their football seriously. A lot of these kids have their hearts set on playing at the college level. They're probably planning to fund college with football scholarships."

Laura pictured the fervor with which some of the parents were shouting at the players to run faster, tackle harder, play smarter. She sighed, "I guess testing the powder wouldn't hurt. I think it's great you've acquired the skills to do it."

Bridget swelled with pride for a moment, then her expression became thoughtful. "I wonder if the assault culprit is a member of the team they played the night the QB was attacked. Maybe someone who figured if he could stop the Loons here, his team wouldn't have to face them in the district final."

"Will that other team be in the district final?"

"It probably depends on if they won their own qualifier game tonight," Bridget said.

Laura found the Loons' game schedule on a far wall and scanned the list, refreshing her memory about how teams made their way through the complicated tournament system. If a team's regular season record was good enough, they would advance to the district, then regional, then state tournament, each one with its own single-elimination system. The goal, of course, was to become state champions.

"It would seem more logical that one of the Marauders attacked the QB, since losing today's game shuts them out of the tournament." Laura tapped the name on the schedule. "Maybe one of them came to our last game prepared to target the QB of whichever team won, since that's who they'd face today."

"If that's the case, Parish couldn't be clueless. The guys would've boasted about it."

"Maybe," Laura said. "But Parish would have made a point of ignoring them because he wouldn't want to know, or at least appear to have known."

"Even if he did know," Bridget said.

"Exactly."

Bridget straightened, apparently satisfied that she'd collected all the evidence she could find. "It'd be good if it turns out to be one of the Marauders. Now that they're shut out, they'd have nothing to gain from trying anything else."

Laura furrowed her brow, a dark thought prickling the back of her neck as she thought about the fight she'd overheard between Bassett and Parish. Sure, the Marauders wouldn't have anything to gain as a team—but their bitter coach might get the revenge he could be seeking.

3

Within an hour of Bread on Arrival's opening Monday morning, the bakehouse was abuzz with customers speculating about who'd been behind the itching powder prank. Laura stood at the front counter with Molly, Carol, and a lingering Trent, who had stopped by for breakfast and stayed to chat when Laura found a free minute.

Next in line and listening to all the chatter, town librarian Grizela Duff sniffed loudly. The stout, gray-haired native Scot was never short on opinions. "Given how unkind the players are to their equipment manager, it wouldn't surprise me in the least if he finally got back at them. I wouldn't blame him either, although its timing was in poor taste."

"I don't think it was Brendan," Veronica Drummond, the community center director, chimed in from the table where she was enjoying a cinnamon scone. "He works at the community center with the kids' programs in the summer. He's a really nice boy. I can't see him retaliating against the team like that."

"Besides being nice," Laura said, "he was the first person the coach blamed for not monitoring the equipment more closely. Seems to me if he was clever enough to mastermind a prank like that to get revenge, he wouldn't get himself into trouble."

"That too," Veronica agreed. "If I had to guess at who was behind the prank, I'd suspect players' ex-girlfriends or guys who've been cut from the team. There are usually one or two players disciplined for bad behavior or failing to maintain their grade point average."

"What about the running back who was dropped to second string after Henry's arrival?" Trent asked Laura. "He was in my shop last week and I couldn't help but overhear him complaining to his buddy about the 'raw deal' he got."

Coach Nelson, the teacher Laura had witnessed arguing with Coach Bassett outside the locker room, stepped up to the counter beside Trent. "That's Ben Merrells. He might have a crack at being an average player if he got rid of the huge chip on his shoulder."

"What do you mean?" Laura asked, suddenly concerned this boy might take out his hostilities on her nephew.

"Nothing is ever his fault," Nelson explained.

Trent's eyes glowed with interest. "My shop assistant, who was at the game, said that unlike the other players, Ben didn't appear to be plagued by the itch."

"Really?" Laura hadn't thought to ask her nephew if any players hadn't been affected. "Were there others who weren't?"

Trent shrugged noncommittally. "I heard there might have been two or three others who also escaped unscathed."

"So any one of them could have been behind the prank," Molly speculated. "But did any of them have motive?"

"I guess that's something we'll need to find out," Laura muttered as much to her friends as to herself. She made a mental note to ask her nephew who else wasn't affected by the powder.

"It wouldn't have bothered me much if the prank lost them the game," a dark-haired, middle-aged woman put in from her spot in line beside Coach Nelson.

Carol grimaced. "Where's your school spirit?" Her frown deepened as she examined the speaker. "Aren't you a teacher?"

"I am." The chastised woman ducked her head. "I know it sounds terrible, and it's not that I didn't want the win for the school. It's what it's costing the rest of our teams. I'm the field hockey coach and my girls desperately need new uniforms, but any expendable funding is being sucked up by the football team to cover the expense of attending the extra tournaments."

"Actually, Kelly, I did hear some good news on that front," Coach Nelson said. "One of the students' parents owns a local nursery and has offered to sell the school hundreds of poinsettias below wholesale prices to resell as a fundraiser." He locked eyes with Carol, Molly, and Laura. "Can we count on you to buy some for the shop?"

"Of course," they said in unison.

"I'll ask Henry to bring home an order form," Laura added.

Nelson cringed.

"Let me guess," Kelly said with a wry smile. "The money students raise will be directed to their sport of choice?"

Coach Nelson huffed. "I'm still trying to convince the athletic director it should be pooled and used where most needed."

The field hockey coach snorted. "Either way, my girls are likely to be overlooked. You don't get college scouts dropping by to watch a field hockey game."

Molly handed the woman the biscuit she'd requested. "I suppose that's true. I don't think I've ever seen a field hockey game."

The woman sighed. "I think that can be said of most of the residents of Loch Mallaig."

Molly pressed her lips together, clearly hesitant to say anything more.

Laura busied herself rearranging the items in a display case as the coaches paid Molly for their purchases. Trent moved to stand on the other side of the case from her, apparently having been waiting for the opportunity to catch her by herself. He favored his mother's Greek heritage with his dark hair, but had his Scottish-American father's green eyes. Laura had decided she was definitely partial to the mix.

"I missed you this weekend," he said. "Can I take you out to dinner tonight?"

Laura started to respond with a smile, then she faltered. "Normally, I'd love to." She sighed. "I think I need to be extra available for Henry right now. At least until we make sure Saturday's prankster doesn't intend to try something else."

"I understand," Trent said, but the light in his eyes had dimmed.

"Rain check?" Laura asked, hoping to reassure him.

He brightened instantly. "Of course. Anytime." He checked his watch, then grabbed the to-go coffee he'd been nursing. "I'd better get to the shop." After saying goodbye to Molly and Carol as well, he trailed the high school coaches out of the bakehouse.

"It'd be sad to think a fellow student would sabotage his own school's chance of winning," Molly said.

"I suppose we can't take anything for granted though," Carol said.

Once school and work started for the day, traffic in the shop slowed to its usual Monday hum. Molly, who handled the bakehouse's marketing efforts, fixed her attention on planning Thanksgiving ads and updating social media posts online while Carol and Laura brainstormed desserts and other baked goods they'd be offering to customers for Thanksgiving.

As they were discussing pumpkin pies and dinner rolls, Laura struggled to stay focused on their conversation. Truth be told, her thoughts were back at Saturday's game, visualizing every detail she could remember in an effort to divine the prankster.

"Earth to Laura," Carol said.

Laura blinked. "Sorry, Carol. I can't stop thinking about the game. What did you say?"

"I asked what you thought about offering a cranberry pecan pie in addition to our traditional recipe." Carol tilted her head. "But since you're so distracted by Loch Mallaig High, I had another idea for our November offerings."

"What's that?"

"We should make cupcakes and cookies frosted with the school colors. With the football team moving on to the district finals, anything that shows team spirit is bound to be popular. Don't you think?"

"That's a great idea. And I think we have a duck-shaped cookie cutter. Close enough to a loon, I think."

"We can do the background in gold and pipe the details in green."

"Love it," Laura said, feeling a rush of gratitude that Carol was a smart businesswoman and a great friend all in one. "I'll make a test batch this morning."

By lunchtime, Laura had a tray full of team spirit cookies ready to display. Officer Dalziel Murdoch, the police department's youngest patroller, arrived at the counter just as Laura was slipping the tray into the display.

"Cool idea," he said to Carol, who was manning the register. "I'll take two and a coffee."

An attractive blonde that Laura didn't recognize sidled up beside him, filling the space surrounding them with an orange blossom fragrance. "Are you a Loon?" she asked with a giggle, squeezing the officer's forearm with her perfectly manicured hand.

Murdoch blinked a few times, confusion flashing in his brown eyes. He glanced from the woman's face to the cookies. "Oh," he said finally. "Yeah. I was. You?"

"No." The blonde shook her head. "I'm Beth Templeton, the school's newest substitute teacher."

"I see." Officer Murdoch was a handsome man in uniform, so Laura assumed women flirted with him often, but she wasn't surprised that the somewhat nervous, though very competent, officer was uneasy about Beth's obvious interest.

Clearly not dissuaded, Beth nudged his arm with her elbow. "I imagine an athletic guy like yourself played football in high school." She surveyed him admiringly from head to toe. He was slender and not particularly tall, but he was obviously fit.

Murdoch's cheeks flared crimson. "I was a kicker."

Beth's smile remained steady. "Then with all your inside knowledge of the team's inner workings, I'm sure it won't take you long to figure out who was behind the assault on our players."

His Adam's apple bobbed as he swallowed. "You mean the itching powder?"

"Of course," Beth said. "I imagine you've already narrowed in on one or two prime suspects."

Patrons sitting at nearby tables grew quiet, apparently waiting on the young officer's response. As Carol set his order on the counter, the crinkling of the paper bag was the only sound.

"Actually, no ma'am." Murdoch cleared his throat. "Such a prank isn't police business."

A collective groan sounded from the dining area.

"Perhaps not, but it's important to the people of Loch Mallaig," Beth pressed, batting her eyelashes. "I mean, if the team hadn't rallied, the prank could've cost them their spot in the district finals."

Laura had tried to stay out of the conversation, but before she could stop herself, she spoke up. "Couldn't you at least question the coach and players?" she asked. "If the culprit sees that his prank has stirred the interest of our local police, maybe he'll think twice before he tries anything else."

Officer Murdoch's expression was skeptical. "I doubt he would try to get away with a second prank."

"What if you're wrong?" Beth asked, sounding as if lives could hang in the balance. She touched the police insignia patch on his arm.

"Solving the mystery would certainly earn you the recognition a man of your obvious capabilities deserves."

The color in Murdoch's cheeks crept to the tips of his ears, even as he seemed to gain a little starch in his spine. "I suppose there'd be no harm in checking into the incident."

The patrons in the dining area broke into applause, and Laura almost felt sorry for the young officer. He was out of his depth with the likes of Beth Templeton, and now he had to live up to the expectations of the entire town, or at least the handful of citizens who had witnessed the exchange.

"Your order is on the house," Laura said, sending Carol a brief glance. "And if there's anything we can do to help, don't hesitate to ask."

"That goes double for me." Beth squealed. "This is wonderful!"

Murdoch smiled uneasily. "Thanks."

Beth checked her watch. "Oh, look at the time. I have to get back for class, but I can meet you after school." She hurried to the door without ordering anything. She paused at the threshold and wiggled her fingers at the officer before slipping out.

Hamish stood up from where he'd been fixing a loose chair leg in the café area. "Well, lad," he said loud enough for all to hear, "I'd say that lass is sweet on you."

Murdoch frowned. "That's the first time I've met her."

"That may be," Hamish said with a chuckle, "but you clearly made an impression."

The officer squirmed. "Excuse me. I need to get back to work."

The instant the door closed behind Murdoch, Laura shot Hamish a smirk. "You're incorrigible."

"I call it like I see it."

"One thing's for sure," Carol said. "If Murdoch uncovers the team's prankster, he'll win more than Beth's adoration. He'll have the whole town's."

"That's true," Laura agreed. "Did something about Beth's request come off as—"

"Flirtatious?" Carol filled in.

"Guileless?" Hamish proposed.

"Desperate?" Sharon Bruce, Hamish's sister-in-law, put in from her table.

"No." Laura shook her head. "I mean, yes. It was those. But it also struck me as . . ." She snapped her fingers until the word came to her. "Manufactured." She stared at the door, replaying the scene between Beth and Murdoch, unable to shake the feeling that the substitute teacher was up to something—and it might not be entirely innocent.

4

Laura cleaned up the bakery's kitchen early so she could catch Henry's football practice from the beginning. Bridget rushed in waving a piece of paper as Laura shelved the last of the baking sheets.

"I've got the test results," Bridget announced. "Want to go with me to share them with Coach Bassett?"

"Absolutely." Laura let Molly and Carol know she was ducking out early, then drove Bridget to the high school.

The sky was a dull gray, threatening drizzle, and the gusty wind made short work of stripping the remaining leaves from the trees dotting the schoolyard. Laura navigated her red Volkswagen Beetle into a cramped space between a souped-up Mustang convertible with the top defiantly down and a black pickup riding on tires so large she would have needed a ladder to climb into the thing.

"Do you know that woman?" Bridget asked after she squeezed out of the car, being careful not to bang the door against the shiny black truck. She pointed to a blonde hurrying across the parking lot toward them.

"She's Beth Templeton, a substitute teacher here," Laura said. "Earlier today, she asked Officer Murdoch to investigate the itching powder incident."

Bridget snorted. "Bet that went over well."

Laura laughed humorlessly. "You'd be surprised. Let's just say Miss Templeton can be quite persuasive." Laura batted her eyelashes to mimic Beth's request.

"Ah."

"Yoo-hoo!" Beth called out. Catching up to them, Beth leaned over to catch her breath. "Have you heard from Officer Murdoch? Do you know if he's coming?"

"Sorry, but I don't," Laura told her.

"Then why are you here?" The woman's petulant tone made her sound like a preteen instead of in her midtwenties.

"To watch my nephew's practice," Laura said at the same time Bridget said, "To talk to Coach Bassett about the test results on the itching powder."

Beth's eyes widened. "You tested the powder? Have you shared the results with Officer Murdoch?"

"Not yet," Bridget said. "I only recently learned he was investigating the incident."

"What did you find?" Beth demanded.

Standing behind Beth, Laura caught Bridget's attention and shook her head.

"I think Coach Bassett should be the first to hear, don't you?" Bridget said. "I haven't even told Laura yet. You're welcome to join us."

Beth waved off the suggestion. "That's okay. I'll wait here to keep an eye out for Officer Murdoch."

Bridget shrugged. "Suit yourself."

The coach was already putting the team through their paces when Laura and Bridget reached the football field. Henry waved to Laura from his position on the thirty-yard line.

The cheerleaders practicing near the grandstands chanted, "Henry, Henry, he's our man! If he can't score, no one can!"

Laura chuckled, recognizing the voice of Moira Blakely, a girl from the St. Andrew's Church youth group, leading the cheer—no doubt for Laura's benefit. Laura saluted their way. "Doing great, girls."

"Coach Bassett, could we have a few minutes of your time?" Bridget asked.

Bassett scowled. "What is it? As you can see, I'm busy."

"I thought you'd be interested to learn that I determined how the itching powder was made," Bridget said.

The coach's expression sharpened. "Oh?"

"It was homemade from the fine silvery hairs of maple keys," Bridget explained. "And there were no traces of it in the opponents' locker room."

"Is that so?" Bassett said.

"It seems unlikely that a man like Coach Parish would take the time to make his own itching powder," Laura added. "He'd simply buy it."

Bassett's eyes narrowed. "Maybe."

Beth hurried toward them with Officer Murdoch trailing in her wake. "Have you learned anything that will help Dalziel—I mean Officer Murdoch—put an end to these pranks?"

Coach Bassett slapped the clipboard he held against his thigh. "It doesn't matter what the powder was made from. It was just a prank, and ultimately the best team won."

Murdoch cleared his throat. "You're more cavalier about the incident than I would've expected, given that it could have cost you a shot at State."

Bassett shook his head. "Trust me, Marcus Parish was behind it. And since I've called him out, he won't dare try anything like that again. Now if you'll excuse me, I need to focus on getting my team ready for district finals."

"I guess that's that then," Officer Murdoch said with a finality akin to washing his hands of the matter.

Beth touched his arm. "You should speak to Marcus. I've taught at his new school. I could introduce you." She gazed up at the officer, her eyes as pleading as the tone of her voice.

"I suppose there's no harm in questioning him," Murdoch agreed, and the pair left.

Laura shifted her attention from the departing couple to Coach Bassett, who was barking instructions to his players on the field.

"Are you okay?" Bridget asked.

"Don't you think the coach should be worried?" Laura shook her head. "Someone clearly went to great lengths to pull the prank, considering how long it must've taken to make itching powder from scratch. What if he doesn't intend to call it quits?"

"I wouldn't be so quick to assume it was a guy," Moira Blakely said, coming up behind them. The pretty cheerleader ducked her head. "Sorry. I didn't mean to startle you, but I couldn't help overhearing."

"You think a girl was behind the prank?" Bridget asked.

Moira shrugged. "Football players have a reputation for being too into themselves for a reason. They think they're God's gift to women as it is. Add their latest winning streak to the mix, and their heads swell to the size of a beach ball."

Laura frowned.

"Don't worry," Moira said reassuringly. "Your nephew doesn't seem at all conceited."

"But I know what you mean," Bridget said. "I've seen some of the college jocks act like that. They can be total jerks to anyone who isn't either a fellow player or a cheerleader."

"Yeah," Moira agreed, "especially to the geeks or the girls who have more brains than beauty—the kind of kids who'd know how to make their own itching powder."

"And who'd like nothing more than to teach them a lesson," Bridget concluded.

Moira nodded. "Exactly."

"Did you have someone particular in mind?" Laura asked.

Moira hesitated, shrugging one shoulder. "I wouldn't want to point fingers."

She didn't have to, because by this time, the rest of the cheerleaders had joined them, and one pointed to an attractive brunette standing by the fence. "Could've been Amy," the newcomer said. "One of the linebackers dumped her a few weeks ago."

Somewhat relieved by Moira's theory, Laura studied Amy, a tall, athletic girl who wore a team jacket that said *Loch Mallaig High School Track and Field*.

Bridget leaned close to Laura and spoke in a low voice. "Isn't she the girl who showed Carol's grandkids how to make helicopters out of maple keys at Saturday's game?"

"You might be right," Laura murmured. "She looks familiar."

"I'm thinking her interest in maple keys might not be a coincidence."

"I kind of hope so." Laura laughed at Bridget's surprise. "With any luck, the itching powder prank has expunged the idea of revenge against her ex from her system."

"Only one way to find out." Bridget smiled conspiratorially. "Shall we go talk to her?"

"She's not going to admit to it," Amy's accuser said derisively.

The team mascot crossed the field with a female teacher, who clapped her hands to gain the cheerleaders' attention. "Why aren't you girls practicing?" she shouted. "Let's go. We want to be in top form for the finals."

Once the cheerleaders had filed away, Bridget jutted her chin toward Amy. "So, do we grill her?"

"I don't know." Laura rolled her neck to slough off the tension that had been building ever since customer speculation over the culprit began that morning—or maybe ever since Saturday's game, if she was honest with herself. "As much as I didn't like that other cheerleader's attitude, she's probably right about at least one thing. If Amy did pull the prank, she's not likely to own up to it. Not unless we can confront her with something more incriminating than the fact that we saw her holding maple keys in a parking lot full of them."

"We should keep our eye on her at least," Bridget suggested. "Because the way I see it, if she's not dating a football player anymore, why is she hanging around their practices? Unless she's up to something."

"Couldn't hurt." Laura redirected her attention to where Henry was practicing on heavy equipment meant to mimic tough linemen. He appeared far more vulnerable than he should for a guy who was bulked out in shoulder pads and a helmet.

Henry pushed through the multiarmed power blaster, then plowed into the heavy hanging dummy. Laura cringed at the force with which her nephew smacked the thing, which was likely filled with a hundred pounds of sand. Digging his feet into the soft earth, Henry drove the equipment down the rail—but the hefty dummy didn't stop at the end. It whizzed off its support arm and crashed to the ground, taking Henry with it.

Behind Laura, the cheerleaders and mascot laughed, along with several of the players.

Laura expected her nephew to roll over and leap to his feet, then give her his huge grin and thumbs-up, but he didn't move from where he'd landed. With a growing sense of horror, Laura wondered if the prankster had struck again—this time with truly terrible consequences.

As the seconds ticked by, Laura resisted the impulse to run to her nephew. Did this kind of thing happen a lot? The last thing she wanted to do was embarrass him with mollycoddling.

Bridget confirmed her fears when she whispered, "I don't think that's supposed to happen."

All of a sudden, Henry let out a loud groan and rolled onto his side but didn't pick himself up. Coach Bassett and his assistant dropped their clipboards and raced toward him. Laura sprinted after them with Bridget on her heels.

Bassett knelt beside Henry and asked how many fingers he was holding up. Somehow, Laura managed to stand back a couple of feet, holding her midriff and her breath as they both waited for his response.

"Three." Henry pushed onto his elbows with a scarcely contained wince. "Ugh, that really knocked the wind out of me."

Behind him, the assistant coach examined the equipment. "The bolt that should've been holding the bumper stopper is gone," he reported. He crouched down beneath the empty screw hole and ran his fingers through the grass, searching for the missing bolt. "I'm not seeing it." He sounded seriously disturbed now. "If it worked its way loose, it should be here."

"What are you saying?" Bassett demanded.

The assistant frowned, his brow knit with worry. "It's been tampered with."

5

Laura's attention snapped to the fence, but Amy was gone.

"Why would she target Henry?" Laura muttered, searching the street beyond the fence for the lithe brunette she'd foolishly imagined couldn't possibly pose any serious danger to her nephew's well-being.

Bridget tracked the direction of Laura's gaze. "Who, Amy? She wouldn't, but Moira said her ex was a linebacker, so he could've been the intended target—except that she'd have no way of knowing when the dummy would give way." Bridget gestured to the field, where Henry still lay on the ground, talking to his coach. "And that's if the bolt was actually removed and didn't just fall out."

The assistant coach was combing through the grass as if he hadn't ruled out that possibility either.

Admittedly, the equipment took a lot of abuse. Laura stuffed her hands in her pockets and willed her feet to stay planted, when everything in her wanted to hug Henry close.

The coach tugged Henry to his feet and clapped him on the back. "Go get yourself a drink."

No longer able to hold herself back, Laura surged forward. "You're okay?"

"He took a hit, but he's tough," Bassett said.

"I'm fine, Aunt Laura." Henry accepted a water bottle from Brendan, wincing on contact, then headed toward the bench.

"Is his wrist okay? Maybe I should take him to the clinic to be sure," Laura murmured to Coach Bassett.

His face scrunched, clearly communicating his opinion—that she was being an overprotective worrywart—but he said only, "He's encountered a lot worse than that in our games this season." He caught the arm of the passing equipment manager. "Hold it there, Brendan. I want a word with you."

Laura scrutinized the rails of the hanging dummy while Bassett grilled Brendan on his inspections schedule. "You're supposed to be checking the equipment," he growled. The lad flinched but stood his ground, apparently used to the coach's temper flares. "Now get inside and see if maintenance has a bolt we can use to repair this."

Laura rejoined Bridget beside the field. "Do you think Brendan would've loosened the bolt?" Laura asked quietly.

Bridget wrinkled her nose. "I doubt it. Although if that's the way the coach and team regularly treat him, I sure wouldn't blame him. But why pull a prank that piles more accusations on his head?"

Brendan shuffled toward the school, his head down, his hands fisted at his sides. The loon mascot trotted across the field after him and slung a feathered wing around his shoulder.

"At least someone's nice to the guy," Bridget murmured. "We'd better get back to the stands. We're in the way here."

Laura's eye skimmed over the dummy still lying on the ground. Something odd caught her eye. She strode forward and squatted down, then pried a torn bit of black nylon fabric from a metal clamp at the top of the dummy. As she examined it, Bridget joined her.

"The Marauders' team jackets are made of that same fabric," Bridget observed. "Maybe one of them decided to get a little payback after their loss on Saturday."

"Maybe. It also looks like the track team jacket Amy was wearing this afternoon." Laura squinted toward the street once more, then toward the school. "Do you think the principal could convince his counterpart at Meadowford High to inspect all his players' jackets for tears?"

"The players' jackets?" Bridget asked. "Or the coach's?"

"Both."

"Given the school's history with Marcus Parish, the principal might prefer to let it slide. After all, beating them was the best revenge."

"As long as they don't try anything else."

Henry approached Laura and Bridget, his backpack slung over his shoulder. "Coach said I could leave early. My wrist is kind of bothering me."

Laura stuffed the scrap of fabric in her pocket for the time being. "I should take you in for an X-ray." At his eye roll, she added, "To be on the safe side."

After confirming Bridget was happy to walk the few blocks home, Laura and Henry headed for her car. Laura noticed the blonde girl who'd come to Brendan's defense Saturday sitting behind the wheel of a dark sedan with a Superior Bay College parking pass hanging from the rearview mirror. She was watching them but abruptly dropped her gaze to her lap rather than meet Laura's eyes.

"Do you know who that is?" Laura asked Henry.

"Brendan's sister, Tina," he answered. "She picks him up after practice. She usually sits in her car and studies until he comes out."

"That's nice of her."

"You're telling me. I would've heard nonstop griping if Adina had to do that for me. She complained enough if Mom asked her to drop me off at the mall on her way somewhere."

"Yeah, your dad was the same with me when we were in school." Laura squinted through the driver's side window as they passed. The girl did have a textbook open on her lap. Then again, hanging around the school so much would give her plenty of opportunity to pull the pranks, and since it sounded as if her brother has been picked on a lot, she had motive. Laura hesitated, but ultimately resisted the temptation to stop and question her. Having Henry's arm seen to was more important.

Two hours later, a doctor declared Henry's wrist merely twisted, not sprained or broken. She sent Laura and Henry on their way with advice to rest and apply ice for a few days.

"What a relief," Laura said as they drove home. "I'd never have heard the end of it from your father if you'd missed the finals because of a broken wrist."

Henry flashed her the grin of a teen who thinks he's invincible.

She wished she shared his confidence. "Bridget mentioned your quarterback was attacked last week."

Henry's lips pursed. "I shouldn't have told her about that."

"Actually, you should have told me. Do you think the guy who attacked him could have swiped the bolt from the equipment you were using?" Laura asked.

Henry shrugged.

"Does your coach know about the attack?" she pressed, wondering how the coach could not be worried, given there had now been three incidents involving his players, two of them in less than a week.

"Jason didn't want to make a big deal about it."

Translation: the coach doesn't know. Laura shook her head. "But what if it is a big deal? Being sixteen doesn't make you indestructible. Today's accident could've been a lot worse." She second-guessed her decision to not speak to the principal immediately. "If that equipment *was* sabotaged, as your assistant coach seemed to think, the saboteur needs to be stopped before someone is seriously hurt."

"Saboteur?" Henry laughed. "You're getting worked up over nothing. The equipment gets a lot of abuse. The bolt could've just fallen out."

"You don't think Brendan would've loosened it?"

"Not a chance. More likely someone who wanted to get *him* into trouble."

Laura thought about that. Bridget had pretty much come to the same conclusion as to why she didn't think he was behind the loosened bolt.

"Brendan gets picked on a lot," Henry added.

"I noticed." And the coach certainly didn't set a good example for his players. She thought about Moira's theory. "Is there anyone else the guys pick on a lot? Maybe a brainy girl or boy?"

"No clue. I don't hang with my teammates outside of practice."

"From what I've heard about some of their behavior, that's probably a good thing." Laura steered her car into the driveway of the old crofter's cottage she rented. It had a view of Loch Mallaig, the town's namesake lake. Today, the tumultuous waves pounding the shore mirrored her thoughts. Boy, had she been naive to think caring for her nephew for the school year would be a piece of cake. She should have known from her years of experience that sometimes baking a successful cake wasn't as easy as it seemed.

When Hamish arrived at the bakehouse the next morning, Laura intercepted him before he could wheel the cart of morning deliveries out to the LaSalle. "Can I ask you something about your days as a history teacher at the high school?"

Hamish raised an eyebrow. "Aye."

"Do you remember where their sports equipment is stored and who has access to it?"

Hamish frowned at what must have been an unexpected question, then scratched his white beard. "There's a large supply closet off the gym with a second door that opens to the outside near the playing fields."

"Is it kept locked?"

"As far as I recall."

"Would any students have a key? For example, a team's equipment manager?"

"No. I assisted the badminton coach one year, and they didn't even issue me a key. Anyone who wants to access the room has to get a coach, an administrator, a gym teacher, or a janitor to open it."

Laura's mind whirled through the list and slammed to a halt at Karl Bassett—the football team's coach, formerly the assistant coach under Marcus Parish. "Do you think the principal would've remembered to ask Marcus Parish to surrender his key when he was fired?"

Hamish's bushy eyebrows arched speculatively. "Bernard Groves runs a tight ship. He wouldn't have forgotten something like that."

"You're certain?"

"Aye. This itching powder incident still eating at you?" he asked as Carol and Molly joined them in the kitchen.

"Or got you scratching your head?" Molly laughed, then grimaced at her own joke. "Sorry. I couldn't resist."

Laura sighed. "It's more than that. Yesterday afternoon, Henry was injured because of an equipment failure."

Molly's mirth instantly changed to concern. "Is he okay?"

"Yes, but it could've been serious," Laura said.

Carol chuckled. "You sound like a regular mother hen."

"And Carol would know," Molly quipped, referring to Carol's brood of laying hens. "I'm sorry, Laura. I know it's not easy. I still remember how it felt the first time Chloe got picked on at school."

Carol nodded. "And it doesn't get any easier. Now I fret over my grandchildren."

Hamish dismissed their fretting with a wave of his hand. "*Dinna fash yersel'* about Marcus. If he shows up at Loch Mallaig High, someone's bound to notice. And as for Henry, he's a football player. Getting hurt goes with the territory."

"You'll get used to it," Molly agreed.

Laura knit her brow. "I don't think I can. You'd better believe I'll keep a keen eye out for interlopers any chance I get."

Hamish snorted but said no more as he pushed the cart loaded with bakery boxes toward the back door.

Even though he was out of earshot, Laura lowered her voice to a conspiratorial whisper. "I was thinking Bread on Arrival could supply some freshly baked protein bars for the players at the next game."

Carol grinned, a knowing glint in her eyes. "It sounds like a good way to gain closer access to the field and locker rooms."

"Exactly." Laura tapped the recipes she'd printed for the purpose. "It'll put me right where I need to be to watch for mischief-makers."

Hearing her nephew's voice at the front of the bakery, Laura glanced at the clock. Lunchtime already? She wiped her hands and grabbed the plate of sample protein bars she'd baked that morning. Emerging from the kitchen, she overheard a couple of his teammates snicker over a girl in the line ahead of them. Laura flashed Henry a censuring look.

Henry immediately tapped his teammates on their backs—the teammates he'd claimed not to hang with, Laura noted. "Hey guys, be nice. This is my aunt's place, remember."

Laura grimaced. She appreciated him taking the initiative to rein in his friends, but it would've been nice if he'd done so out of common decency rather than the threat of getting in trouble with his aunt. She waved Henry and his friends over to the side counter. "I thought the bakehouse might donate some snacks to your team for the next tournament. Would you boys like to taste test them?"

They whooped and descended on the plate. The samples disappeared instantly.

"Those were fantastic," one of the boys said. His teammates echoed the sentiment, and Henry thanked her with a genuine smile on his face.

"My pleasure," Laura said.

The guys left without buying anything—not that Laura should be surprised after giving them free food—leaving the customer line empty. The girls who'd been in line ahead of the players—Brendan's sister, Tina, included—had taken their drinks and pastries to a nearby table. The second the shop door swung closed behind Henry, they launched into a group diatribe about their contempt for football players.

"If you ask me," said one of the girls, a mousy brunette with a long ponytail and thick-rimmed glasses, "they deserved the itching powder."

"Yeah," a girl with black braids agreed. "And their equipment going haywire on them."

Laura fisted her hands and stepped toward them. Her nephew had *not* deserved to get hurt.

Molly must've noticed the steam building in Laura like an expanding soufflé, because she whipped around the counter and reached the girls ahead of her. "Hi, Tina," Molly said jovially. "Good to see you here."

She smiled at Laura. "This is Tina Lancashire, a junior member of The Piping Yoopers. She plays bagpipes better than I do."

Laura pressed her lips together to contain the lecture straining to burst out.

Molly lowered her voice and leaned toward Tina. "I was wondering what the reason might be for all this hostility toward the football team."

Tina's eyes flared. "Brendan, the team's equipment manager, or water boy, or whatever you want to call him, is my little brother. I hate the way the players and even the coaches treat him."

Laura's righteous indignation shrank a fraction. "You should be proud of him. I was impressed by how courageously he turned the other cheek when Coach Bassett blamed him for the itching powder in the players' shoulder pads."

Tina snorted. "Guaranteed neither the coach nor his players had their consciences the least bit pricked."

Laura nodded. The girl was likely right. But was Tina angry enough to seek revenge on her brother's behalf? After seeing how the coach blamed Brendan for the first incident, surely she wouldn't have sabotaged the equipment her brother was responsible for maintaining a second time—would she?

Henry came back to the bakery after school while Laura, Carol, and Bridget were still cleaning up.

"No practice today?" Bridget asked.

"The doctor said I should rest my wrist for a day or two," he answered, his voice a bit sullen. "Can we have my tutoring session early?" He glanced at Laura. "I was hoping it'd be okay if I went to a movie tonight with friends."

"The early show?" Laura asked.

He grinned. "Yeah."

"Then it's okay with me as long as it works for Bridget," Laura said. "Carol and I will finish cleaning if you want to start now. You can even work here."

"Thanks, Laura," Bridget said, then led Henry to a table, where he fished out his math and English textbooks from his backpack.

A little while later, the scrape of a key in the bakehouse's front door brought Laura surging to her feet from behind the counter, where she'd been dusting the bottom shelves.

Molly hobbled in with her adorable Scottish terrier, Angus, both appearing quite bedraggled.

"What happened to you?" Laura asked as she came into the café area.

"After we delivered the ad copy to the newspaper, we happened upon a couple of large dogs that had a cat cornered," Molly said.

"Let me guess." Carol snapped shut the napkin dispenser she'd been in the process of filling. "Angus gave the bullies their comeuppance."

"He sure did." Molly stooped and scratched the dog's ears. "I'm so proud of him. He distracted the dogs long enough for the cat to escape."

"I hope he didn't get hurt, though." Carol gestured to the patch of slobber on Angus's back before stooping to pet him.

"He got away mostly unscathed, aside from a splash of drool." Molly sighed. "Unfortunately, I wasn't quite as brave as him, so it took me a few moments to scrounge up the courage to step into the fray and send the dogs packing."

"Would you have been as brave as Angus if you'd faced a similar situation?" Laura asked her nephew.

"Sure, I guess."

"Have you ever risen to Brendan's defense?"

Henry ducked his head sheepishly. "Not really."

"You haven't picked on him yourself, have you?" Laura pressed.

"No," Henry said. "I already told you."

"Okay." Laura held up her hands. "Just making sure." She only hoped Henry was telling her the truth, not what he thought she wanted to hear.

That evening, Laura's brother, Brody, and his wife, Eliza, called to check in with Henry.

"I'm sorry," she told them. "He went to a movie tonight. But it was the early show and he finished his homework before he left." Of course, the fact didn't stop her insides from squirming over getting caught letting him go out on a school night. Not that there was anything wrong with it. She just wasn't sure if Brody and Eliza would feel the same.

"How's the tutor you found Henry working out?" Brody asked, as unflappable as ever. Then again, he would be, since she'd more or less kept him and Eliza in the dark about the goings-on in Loch Mallaig.

"Really well," she said, glad to have positive news to share. "His grades seem to be improving."

"Terrific," Eliza said. "I knew we could count on you to keep Henry on track."

Before Laura could respond, Brody said, "We got word today that our project will be done the week before Thanksgiving, so we'll be home for the holiday. Eliza can't wait."

Eliza chuckled. "Funny how he doesn't tell you he's the one who misses the kids the most."

Laura smiled. "I'm not surprised." Her grin broadened. "If the Loons make the state finals, you could make it home in time for the game."

"Wouldn't that be something?" Brody gushed. There was no mistaking the pride in his voice. It must be killing him to miss out on seeing his son play. "I'm glad Karl recognized Henry's talent. Henry's coach back home didn't seem to like him much and rarely played him."

Laura's ears perked up at Brody's familiar tone. "Wait, you know Karl Bassett?"

"Sure," he said. "We lived in the same dorm sophomore year."

"You never mentioned that before." Laura couldn't help but wonder if her brother's sending Henry to live with her had as much to do with her proximity to Karl's school as the fact she was his aunt.

"How's Henry doing?" Eliza asked.

"Good." Laura's heart thumped as she wrestled with her conscience over how much to say, if anything, about the attacks on the team. She settled on, "He did twist his wrist during practice yesterday, but the doc said he'll be good as new by the weekend." Before they could weigh in, she asked, "How's the mission going so far?"

While Brody talked, headlights flashed as a car navigated into Laura's driveway. Laura rose to peek past the curtain and recognized Fergus's SUV. What was he doing here? Molly jumped out of the passenger side door, followed by—

Laura squinted at the young man. Henry?

Barely listening to Brody, Laura dashed to the door and flicked on the porch light. Swinging the door wide, she was about to tell her brother Henry had arrived when she caught a glimpse of her nephew's face. His left eye was swollen and three shades of blue.

How had Henry gotten a black eye?

6

After quickly disconnecting from her brother—she'd explain later when she herself knew what was going on—Laura ushered Henry, Molly, and Fergus into the cottage. "What happened?" she asked, then held up a hand. "Just a minute. Let me get an ice pack for that eye first."

Laura dashed to the kitchen and cracked a tray of ice cubes into a plastic bag, then wrapped it in a clean dish towel. She returned to the living room and handed the ice pack to Henry, who'd sprawled on the armchair. Molly and Fergus perched on the edge of the sofa.

"Explain," Laura ordered, hands on her hips.

Henry gingerly held the ice to his eye. "This is what I get for coming between fighting dogs."

"Fighting dogs?" A memory of Molly's afternoon adventure materialized in Laura's mind. "You stood up for Brendan?"

Henry shrugged. "Can I go to my room?"

Laura shot Molly a helpless glance, and Molly mouthed, "Let him go."

Laura reluctantly consented. The instant his bedroom door clicked shut, Molly grew animated. "Fergus and I ran into Henry and his girlfriend outside the movie theater."

"Wait," Laura said, confused. "What girlfriend? He said he was going to the movies with friends. I assumed he meant guy friends."

Fergus chuckled. "No doubt that's what he wanted you to assume."

Laura frowned. The incidents striking Henry's football team were unsettling enough. What was she supposed to do with a lovestruck teen boy sneaking around?

"Oh my," Molly said to Fergus. "She looks like a deer caught in the headlights."

Fergus leaned back and propped his foot on his knee. "Don't sweat it. Having raised both, I can tell you that boys bring less drama to the table than girls when it comes to dating. You can handle this."

Laura's chest tightened. "What, exactly, do I have to handle? Did Henry get into a fight over a girl?"

"From what I could gather," Fergus said, "it sounded as if some punk made a snide comment about Henry's date, so Henry took a swing at him."

"Except that Henry missed," Molly interjected.

"And the punk swung back," Fergus continued. "He managed to land a shot before we could intervene."

"No wonder Henry didn't want to talk about it." Laura stared at her cell phone, abandoned after cutting off her brother midconversation. He was bound to ask why she'd abruptly ended their call. How was she ever going to explain this to him?

Before sunrise the next morning, as Laura tucked the sandwiches she'd made for Henry into his lunch bag, Henry ambled into the kitchen holding his stomach.

"What are you doing up so early?" Laura asked.

"My stomach is killing me," he replied. "I think I need to stay home from school today."

His eye now sported three additional shades of purple and blue, and Laura suspected the only thing bothering Henry's stomach was the thought of being seen this way. She retrieved a mug from the cupboard, plopped in a peppermint tea bag and poured water from the already-hot kettle over it. "Let this steep for a few minutes, then drink it and go back to sleep for a while. Your alarm clock won't go off for two more hours. I'm sure you'll feel much better by then."

He accepted the mug but studied its contents skeptically. "If I don't, I'll stay home, okay? The school may call you to ask why I'm not there."

Ah, so that's why he didn't conveniently miss the bus after I left for work. Studying him, Laura sipped her own tea. "It'd be a shame for you to miss school. When all the girls hear you got that black eye by defending your date's honor, they'll be swooning in the aisles."

Henry brightened. "Really?"

"That's my guess." She set down her empty cup. "And for the record, next time you want to go on a date, you can just tell me."

His chin dipped. "That's cool. Thanks. And, um, maybe I will try to make it to class. I wouldn't want to miss another football practice. Coach might drop me from the starting lineup."

"We wouldn't want that," Laura agreed.

She did her best to ignore the small voice at the back of her mind reminding her that practice might not be the safest place for Henry to be, but it pestered her all day—to the point where she knew she couldn't stay out of it. She recruited Molly, Fergus, and Carol to accompany her to Henry's practice after closing time, and Molly brought Angus along to help them sniff out trouble. The team was already on the field when they arrived.

Carol pointed to Coach Bassett shaking the padded metal arms of the power blaster. "At least he's double-checking the equipment."

"That's a relief," Laura said.

Fergus motioned toward the boy lugging out a sack of footballs. "Is that Brendan?"

"Yes." Laura noticed that the players barely acknowledged the boy as they each accepted a ball. "Wouldn't hurt for them to say thank you."

"The coach should encourage his team to be nicer," Molly said.

"Yes, he should," Laura muttered. *Except Coach Bassett was as unkind to him as the players, if not more so.* She spotted the stout, balding principal coming out of the school. "You guys have a seat on the bleachers." She stuck her hand into her purse and pulled out the scrap of black fabric she'd untangled from the dummy. "I need to speak to Mr. Groves for a moment."

Before Laura could intercept him, Mr. Groves caught up to Coach Bassett. "A grievance has been filed against the team," the principal declared, clearly aggravated. "Someone claims you brought Henry Donovan in as a ringer."

Laura sucked in a sharp breath at the mention of her nephew.

A nearby player grinned. "Does this mean I get my place back on first string?"

Laura studied the teen, guessing he must be Ben Merrells, the player the track-and-field coach had mentioned.

Bassett scowled at the lad. "There's no way the claim will stand, Merrells. Henry legitimately transferred here to live with his aunt." The coach lifted his chin toward Laura, who felt like an eavesdropper hovering so close by. "Isn't that right, Ms. Donovan?"

"Yes." She stepped closer. "My brother and his wife are on a church mission trip out of the country. They offered Henry the choice between staying with me and attending Loch Mallaig High, or going to South America with them."

Laura swallowed a sudden lump in her throat. After last night's conversation with her brother, she couldn't help wondering if he'd somehow cooked up a plan with his old college buddy to create opportunity for Henry to play for Loch Mallaig. Either way, though, Henry was a legitimate transfer student.

The assistant coach cleared his throat. "My guess is Marcus Parish filed this grievance as retaliation over losing last Saturday's game."

Mr. Groves nodded. "That's likely. The oversight committee recognizes his allegations might be motivated by a grudge against our school. He managed to get another team disqualified, which has bumped his school into the division finals. I'm afraid he'll try any angle he can think of to ensure we don't make it through the tournament."

Laura's grip tightened on the implicating scrap of fabric. She thrust it toward Mr. Groves. "I should've brought this to your attention the moment I found it."

Groves took the fabric and examined it, his brow furrowing. "What is it?"

"I found it caught in the dummy mechanism after my nephew's accident. I thought it might have been torn off the clothing of whoever tampered with the bolt. Black nylon is fairly common, though."

Bassett helped himself to the fabric and rubbed it between his fingers. "Could be from one of Meadowford High's team jackets." He slapped the evidence back into the principal's hands. "I knew Parish was behind all this."

"I'll take care of it." Mr. Groves pointed at Bassett. "You focus on coaching. The last thing we want is for this tournament to turn into a mudslinging match. We can rise above all this if cool heads prevail." The coach snorted a response, but the principal flapped a dismissive hand and said, "Carry on," before heading back inside.

"Do you think Marcus Parish will try something else to sabotage the team?" Laura asked Coach Bassett, regretting again that she hadn't shown him the fabric two days before. If she had, being confronted with the evidence might have already put an end to Parish's schemes.

"I'm counting on it." He scowled in the direction of Ben Merrells, now receiving passes from another player. "And I'd say we have a mole in the school. How else could Parish have found out about Henry's school transfer?"

A mole? Laura shook her head as she walked back to the bleachers. She'd had no idea how seriously people took high school football.

"What's going on?" Molly asked when Laura rejoined the group.

Angus glanced up from where he was sniffing a discarded candy wrapper beneath the seats. If he'd been here two days ago, could his nose have told them whose scent was on that scrap of fabric? Laura had assumed it belonged to Parish or one of his players. But what if she'd been right about it belonging to Amy? In addition to having a grudge against the lineman who dumped her, could she be a mole for Parish?

Or was Merrells doing the opposing coach's dirty work? Bassett clearly suspected him, but would Ben really jeopardize his team's chances of winning? Sure, disqualifying Henry might get him back on to first string, but the itching prank could have been the end of their playing season. And the hanging dummy could just as easily have given way when he was using it. He couldn't have been certain Henry would be the one injured.

"Laura?" Molly prodded.

Laura shook the swirling thoughts from her head. "Sorry." She updated the group on the latest development.

Fergus offered a reassuring smile. "Don't worry. Henry will be okay."

Laura sighed. "I hope so. I hate feeling so helpless."

"You, Bridget, and I will be at Friday's game in Houghton," Molly reminded her. "I'm sure between us, we'll be able to scope out any interlopers. I could bring Angus along if you'd like. He is an excellent judge of character."

Laura smiled. "Unfortunately, I don't think he's allowed on the football field." She frowned toward a couple of leather-clad teens loitering behind the bleachers making snide comments about the cheerleaders' attempts to build a human pyramid. "It'd be nice if Angus could scare that lot away. They're the same guys who were belittling the players at Saturday's game."

Molly sized up the pair. "Something tells me my little Scottie doesn't have enough flint in his bark to intimidate those two."

Fergus rose. "Excuse me a minute. I need to stretch my legs."

He sauntered around to the back of the bleachers about the same time one of the boys made a derogatory comment about Moira.

"It's time you lads moved on," Fergus said authoritatively.

"You gonna make us, old man?" one replied with a sneer.

"Just making a suggestion before you get yourselves into trouble," Fergus replied.

"Maybe we like trouble," the other youth said defiantly.

"And do those motorcycles in the parking lot belong to you?" Fergus asked.

"Maybe," the first boy snapped. "What's it to you?"

"There's a cop over there," his friend muttered barely loud enough for Laura to hear.

Laura shifted for a better view of the parking lot and spotted Officer Murdoch and Beth Templeton chatting with Bridget by his cruiser, not far from a pair of motorcycles.

The teens opted to head in the opposite direction and didn't stop until they reached the school fence. They casually leaned back against it, trying to appear tough once more.

"My hero," Molly said, pretending to swoon as Fergus rejoined them in the bleachers.

He grinned and winked at her.

Sensing they'd rather be enjoying a quiet walk along the lake than watching a bunch of rowdy teen boys, Laura said, "You two don't need to stay on my account."

"Yes, Bridget can help us scour the vicinity for trouble," Carol added.

Molly and Fergus didn't argue, but he did slant one last menacing glare in the direction of the leather-clad youths by the fence. As the couple left, they stopped in the parking lot and chatted with Bridget and Officer Murdoch a moment, then Bridget joined Laura and Carol.

"I told Officer Murdoch about the fabric scrap you found," Bridget said. "Fergus told us you gave it to the principal, so Officer Murdoch is going to talk to him. Unfortunately, he hasn't come across any other leads."

"Mom?" Carol's daughter, Jenny, cut across the corner of the field, making her way toward them. She wore a dark skirt and fuchsia blouse that complimented her dark complexion, a chemistry textbook and a folder under her arm. "What are you doing here?"

Carol stood and gave her daughter a warm hug. "I came with Laura to watch the football practice. After Monday's incident, we figured we should keep an eye out for more trouble."

Jenny's brow creased. "You really think someone set out to hurt our players on purpose?"

"I wouldn't discount the possibility." Carol said. After decades of experience teaching math to kids this age, Carol would know what they were capable of doing.

"Have you taught any of the players, Jenny?" Laura asked.

She nodded. "A handful."

"Do you know if any of them were particularly close to their former coach, Marcus Parish?"

Jenny shrugged. "Sorry, but I have no clue."

Laura nodded toward the pair of troublemakers still standing by the fence. "Do you know those guys?"

"The dark-haired one is Frank Aldridge," Jenny said. "He played football last year. He was an average player. He got cut from the team at the beginning of this season after he was caught breaking curfew."

"I think I remember his aunt Pippa fretting about that at a Fair Knitting Ladies meeting," Carol piped up. "Her son is the same age as her nephew, and she said they spend a lot of time together. I wonder if the other lad is him."

"Getting kicked off the team sounds like a motive to mess with them if I ever heard one," Laura said.

"I suppose." Jenny checked her watch. "I'm afraid I have to run. The twins have a piano lesson with Joyce Bruce in twenty minutes."

"Say hi to her for us," Carol said, and Jenny agreed before hurrying toward the parking lot.

With Fergus gone, the pair of troublemakers soon wandered back toward the bleachers.

"I hope that other lad isn't Pippa's son," Carol said.

"Maybe they're our culprits, hiding in plain sight," Bridget said. "They seem brazen enough to presume they're untouchable. Henry said the guy who attacked their QB was wearing a leather jacket."

"He was?" Laura exclaimed. "We should suggest to Officer Murdoch that he have a chat with these boys."

"Absolutely," Carol agreed. "I'll see what I can find out from Pippa at our meeting tomorrow night."

"You'll have to let me know what she says," Laura said. "I should probably skip this week with the tournament starting Friday."

"No problem," Carol assured her.

The leather-clad boys took up a spot where the fence met the bleachers. The taller of the pair, Frank, made a loud, derogatory comment about Moira, who was apparently his ex and also happened to be dating the team's quarterback, Jason.

Though not in his Larry the Loon costume, Kit was practicing with the cheerleaders, and he must have overheard. He said something to Moira, then stalked toward the unruly teens.

"Come to protect your *chicks*?" one of the guys taunted.

Kit crossed his arms over his chest. "Get lost."

"You don't even need a costume to look like a loon," Frank said with a sneer, and the pair laughed.

"At least I don't need to insult nice girls to feel good about myself," Kit said loudly enough for everyone to hear. "She dumped you because you weren't good enough for her."

Several of the football players, Jason included, stopped what they were doing and tuned into the scene at the bleachers.

"I couldn't care less," Frank retorted, though it was clear he certainly did care. He glared at the audience on the field, then slapped his buddy's arm. "Let's get out of here."

Kit resumed his post amid applause from the cheerleaders.

"He's a good egg," Carol said.

"I just hope those goons don't decide to corner him alone in a dark alley," Bridget said. "That's how creeps like that work."

Laura glanced over at Henry with his black eye. *Sometimes they don't even bother to get them alone.*

7

Laura drove to the bakehouse extra early Thursday morning to get ahead on the day's baking. She wanted plenty of time at the front of the shop questioning customers. If Marcus Parish had a mole at Loch Mallaig High, someone in town had to be aware of the connection. Coach Bassett obviously suspected Ben Merrells, but the chip on Frank Aldridge's shoulder seemed even bigger than Ben's.

Carol arrived before six o'clock and gaped at the trays of biscuits, scones, and breads already cooling on trays. "Couldn't sleep?"

"How'd you guess?" Laura asked wryly.

"If it helps, I asked Jenny to keep her ears open for any chitchat about the mischief surrounding the football team. She promised to let me know if she hears anything that might help us catch our culprit."

Laura shot her friend a grateful smile. "Thank you."

By the time Bread on Arrival opened an hour later, Laura had the day's orders boxed and ready for delivery and her last batch of oatcakes in the oven.

She was sliding the final tray of scones into the display case when Doreen Giobsan stepped into the shop. Doreen owned Thistle and That, the gift shop next door. Like many in the town who boasted Scottish heritage, she was blessed with dark red hair, which she wore in a chic, chin-length bob.

"How's that nephew of yours doing, Laura?" Doreen asked. "I heard he had a spot of trouble at football practice Monday afternoon."

Laura wasn't surprised at the question. Doreen always seemed to know the town gossip—which, come to think of it, made her the perfect starting point for an information-gathering mission. "Henry's wrist is still a little sore, I think, but he's not letting it slow him down."

"Good to hear," Doreen said. "The whole town is rooting for our boys to bring home the championship."

Laura tilted her head. "There's at least one person who isn't, wouldn't you say?"

Doreen's eyes sprang wide, then understanding seemed to dawn on her and she laid a finger alongside her nose. "Ah, you mean our itching powder prankster?"

Among other things. "Yes."

"I heard the infamous Marcus Parish was implicated in that."

"He denies the accusation."

"Well, he would, wouldn't he?" Doreen raised an eyebrow. "But he isn't known for being all that truthful."

"I've gotten the impression many people don't trust him," Laura said. "However, there have been a couple of other incidents that appear to be connected, and at least one of them involved a younger perpetrator."

"You don't say!" Doreen leaned over the counter and lowered her voice conspiratorially. "What was that?"

Laura winced, not sure she wanted her suspicions about the connection between the attack on the quarterback and the pranks spread about town. "I'm not at liberty to say at the moment."

Carol walked from the coffee maker to the counter and slid a fresh cup across to Doreen. "Do you happen to know Ben Merrells?"

"Ben Merrells," Doreen repeated thoughtfully. "No, I can't say I do." She raised the cup. "Thanks for this. You read my mind. Can I have a poppy-seed scone too?"

"You've got it," Carol said, then busied herself plating the scone.

"Do you know a girl named Amy?" Laura asked. "I don't know her last name. She was dating one of the team's linebackers until recently."

"Oh yes, I know Amy." Doreen beamed. "Her mother has worked for me part-time over several Christmas seasons. A lovely girl. She's on the track-and-field team and very smart. I suspect she'll be leaving us on an academic scholarship to Michigan State next year."

"That's marvelous," Carol chimed in as she gave Doreen her scone. "What field is she interested in?"

"Chemistry, I think. Your daughter must know her." Doreen sniffed the air. "Is something burning?"

"Oh no, my oatcakes!" Laura dashed away from the counter and down the hall. The kitchen was filled with smoke. Laura fanned the air with a dish towel, then tugged the tray of ruined oatcakes from the oven. She almost never burned anything, and embarrassment outweighed the loss of product as the main consequence of this incident.

Molly poked her head through the door. "Everything okay?"

"The oatcakes aren't, but we don't need to alert the fire department, if that's what you mean."

Molly grinned. "I'm happy to if you think it'd help. Fergus is one of the volunteers on call this week."

Laura rolled her eyes. "I'm sure he'll be in to see you without needing the pretense of a fire call." Then she grinned. She couldn't be truly mad about Molly's happiness. After losing her husband far too young, Molly deserved a second chance at love.

Sighing, Laura pulled out ingredients for oatcakes for the second time that morning. Maybe once this whole football business settled down, she could spend more time with Trent. There was clearly chemistry there, but between his getting his new outfitter's business off the ground and her being responsible for her nephew on top of helping her partners run a successful bakehouse, making time together wasn't as simple as it should be.

Once her new batch of oatcakes was baking, Laura set the timer on her cell phone so she'd hear it while out front grilling customers for information. She arranged a fresh tray of the cookies Carol had decorated in the high school's colors and carried them out to the display case. Most of the first tray had already sold.

Carol nudged Laura's arm as she passed. "Mrs. Baker at the table next to the fireplace is a neighbor of the Aldridges."

"Thanks." Laura slid the tray of cookies into the case, then approached Mrs. Baker, a cheerful retired bank teller with a ready smile. "How are you today?"

"Just grand, dear." Mrs. Baker nodded toward the case Laura had just left. "I must say, those goodies in the school's colors were a smashing idea."

"I'm glad you like them," Laura said. "We're donating a portion of the proceeds from their sale to the school's fundraising efforts."

"Yes, Carol told me." Mrs. Baker set down her coffee mug and patted the bakery box on the table next to it. "That's why I bought a dozen to take home for the neighborhood children. We don't have any grandchildren of our own yet, but my husband likes to referee the games of pickup hockey the kids have in the street after school."

"That's so sweet of you." Seeing her opportunity to segue into talking about Frank Aldridge, Laura took a deep breath. "Does Frank join in on the hockey games?"

"Not that I've seen," Mrs. Baker said. "He used to. Now he's more interested in his motorcycle. It's a shame. He used to be such a nice boy."

"He's not anymore?"

Mrs. Baker's gaze dropped. "Goodness. I shouldn't have said that. What must you think? That's not what I meant. I don't know what he's like now. He still lives next door, but he doesn't stop and chat like he used to when he delivered our newspaper. He got busy with sports once he started high school, but I don't think he plays anymore. I get the sense his mother is pulling her hair out over him more often than not." The woman shook her head. "There I go again. I don't mean to gossip."

"I was the one who asked about him," Laura said. "I met him recently, and I got the sense he was troubled." Laura let her voice trail off, hoping to encourage Mrs. Baker to fill in the blanks.

The older woman sighed. "Teens these days. I don't understand them. I suppose my mother thought I was wild when I was that age, and the worst I ever did was go to a beatnik poetry reading."

Mrs. Baker finished her coffee and Laura excused herself to check on her oatcakes. Thankfully, these were perfectly golden, and Laura was relieved she hadn't ruined the simple recipe for a second time. She got to work on an order of miniature chocolate tortes for a luncheon the next day at Castleglen.

As Laura was pulling the tortes from the oven a while later and swapping them with trays of chocolate chip cookies, Carol cruised in with an empty tray. "Do you need a hand in here? I figure you'll want to be out front when the lunch crowd comes through from the high school."

"I thought I did," Laura said as she pushed the last tray of tortes into a cooling rack. She grabbed a final tray of cookies and slid them into the oven. "But I'm beginning to think we won't learn much this way. How can we be so good at solving murders and so hopeless at unmasking a saboteur?"

Carol hesitated. "Do you think it's possible that maybe there isn't one? We don't know the incidents are connected. The guy who attacked the QB may have had a grudge against him that had nothing to do with football. The incident with the practice equipment could've been an accident caused by regular wear and tear that went unnoticed. The itching powder is the only obviously deliberate prank."

Laura sighed. "Am I worrying for nothing?"

"Honestly, I'm hoping you are. It could be a coincidence." Carol put a hand on Laura's arm. "Why don't you grab yourself a cup of tea and take a break? A mental break too."

Laura made a face but did as Carol suggested. She donned a sweater and took a cup of tea out to the front porch, hoping the sunshine and fresh air would clear her head. A few moments later, a small group of high school students dashed up the front walk. Recognizing Moira, Brendan, and Kit among them, Laura straightened.

All but Kit charged inside without noticing her. He stopped beside her chair. "Hey, you're Henry Donovan's aunt, right?"

"That's right," Laura answered.

"I'm Kit Williams. I heard you were trying to figure out who tampered with the equipment he got hurt on."

"Do you know anything that might help?" she asked.

"I know it wasn't Brendan's fault," Kit said. "The poor guy gets blamed for everything, and he works as hard as anyone else on the team. Maybe harder."

Laura nodded. "I'd gathered that much."

"Merrells is ticked with Henry for getting him bumped from first string, you know."

"I'd heard that. What can you tell me about Frank Aldridge?"

"He'd always been a second-string player, but it's no one's fault but his own that he got cut from the team."

"For his behavior?"

"Yeah. Too bad he can't take the hint and stay away from practices too."

Laura appraised the teen, who had a smattering of acne across his chin amid patchy black stubble that marked the beginnings of a mustache. "I take it you don't like him very much."

"I hate the way he creeps out Moira. Watching her, making snarky remarks. I don't know what she ever saw in the jerk. I mean, she goes to church and he stays out all night doing who knows what."

"Lots of girls are attracted to that type of guy," Laura said, recalling her own teen infatuations with bad boys.

"Good thing Moira was smart enough to cut and run when she did," Kit said.

"Do you think Frank's the kind of guy who would have a go at her new boyfriend?" Laura asked. "Or maybe try to ruin their football season out of spite?"

Kit nodded vigorously. "For sure. You saw what a jerk he was being yesterday afternoon. I wouldn't put anything past him. Come to think of it, besides being a total jerk in the stands with his catcalls at last Saturday's game, I remember seeing him go into the locker rooms. At the time, I figured he was using the bathroom."

"And having used the football equipment," Laura added, "I'm guessing he'd know exactly which bolt would need loosening to cause an accident."

"Totally."

Laura's chest tightened with a combination of exhilaration that her suspicions were being corroborated and anxiety over what the kid might try next.

Moira poked her head out the door. "Are you coming or not, Kit?"

"I'll be right there," Kit said and excused himself.

A hint of acrid smoke and the sound of Angus's bark coming from upstairs wafted through the air with the swing of the door. *The cookies!* Laura dashed through the dining area, past the counter, and down the hall to the kitchen. Molly was already there, waving a towel near the smoke detector to keep it from going off. A tray of blackened cookies sat on the counter.

"Ugh," Laura growled. "I can't believe I let something *else* burn."

"You have a lot on your mind," Molly said sympathetically.

"Clearly not what's supposed to be on it. I completely forgot I'd put the cookies into the oven."

"Angus alerted us before the smoke alarm went off, so I got here before anyone panicked." Molly returned the towel to the rack and gave Laura a sideways hug. "Don't beat yourself up. We can afford to eat the loss." She gingerly pried one of the blackened cookies from the tray and scrunched her nose as she scrutinized it more closely. "Well, maybe not literally eat it. I don't think even Angus would be tempted by these."

Laura chuckled. "If I keep this up, perhaps we can smoke out the culprit."

Molly smiled triumphantly. "If you're making puns, you can't be that upset."

Upset or not, Laura decided for everyone's safety not to risk baking anything else that day. After scraping the burned cookies into the trash and scrubbing the pan, Laura joined Molly out front, where she was serving Beth Templeton and apparently discussing Frank and Moira's breakup.

"I've never understood the attraction to bad boys," Beth said. She glanced around the shop and lowered her voice, adding, "I'm partial to law-and-order types myself."

"Have you heard whether Officer Murdoch questioned Parish about the scrap of fabric I found on the sabotaged equipment?" Laura asked, frustrated that the man hadn't been in the bakehouse himself. He was usually a regular. Was he avoiding her?

"I've heard you three here have a reputation for solving mysteries," Beth said, "but you should leave this one in Officer Murdoch's capable hands." She gave Molly a five-dollar bill and told her to keep the change, then gathered up her bag and coffee and left.

"I guess we've been told," Molly said. "Funny, it's usually the cops telling us to stay out of it."

"Speaking of cops," Carol murmured as she passed the counter on her way to the kitchen with a bus tub. She nodded toward the hallway.

Officer Murdoch had poked his head out of the door marked *Laddies*. "Is she gone?"

"Is who gone?" Carol asked innocently, setting her bus tub on the back counter.

"Miss Templeton," he answered.

"Yes, she just left." Laura tamped down the laughter threatening to bubble out as she grinned at him. She was pretty sure she heard Murdoch breathe a sigh of relief as he joined them at the counter.

"You should ask Beth out," Molly urged. "She's clearly smitten."

Murdoch blushed. "I don't know about that."

"You're not dating anyone else at the moment, are you?" Molly pressed.

"N-no," the officer stammered, clearly uncomfortable. "I don't date much."

Laura felt a rush of sympathy for the shy officer who likely feared rejection. She decided to rescue him and have her own questions answered at the same time. "What did Marcus Parish say when you questioned him, Officer Murdoch?"

"He swore he didn't have anything to do with the itching powder prank," Murdoch answered.

Laura gave him an appraising stare. "Do you believe him?"

"Yes," the officer said. "He told me he wouldn't be surprised if Bassett pranked his own team to save face if they didn't win. The chances of his contract being renewed were slim if the team crashed and burned—unless he could blame extenuating circumstances."

"Do you think he could be right?" Carol asked.

Murdoch shrugged. "The notion that Bassett would sabotage his team before they even started playing to save face if they lost is pretty far-fetched."

"I agree with you on that," Molly said.

"One thing I can tell you," Murdoch went on, "is that Parish was wearing his team jacket when I met with him, and I didn't notice any tears in it."

Laura nodded. That was something, anyway.

After the officer left, Carol continued to the kitchen, and Molly and Laura mulled over the idea of Coach Bassett being responsible for the itching powder prank. "It would explain why he was so quick to dismiss Bridget's test results," Laura said, "but at the end of the day, the theory doesn't hold much water."

"And I can't believe he'd jeopardize a player's safety by sabotaging equipment," Molly said.

"I can't either," Laura agreed.

"So maybe the equipment failure was merely an accident."

"Maybe."

Laura wasn't convinced. She couldn't shake the feeling that someone was out to get the Loch Mallaig Loons—and Henry was going to be caught in the crosshairs.

8

Laura went back to the kitchen. "I'd better mix up some dough for Carol to bake on Saturday morning," she murmured to herself, thinking a late night on Friday might keep her and Molly in bed after their alarms. Her eyes strayed to the clock. It was nearly closing time, and Henry's practice would start soon. Should she go keep an eye on him again instead of making dough?

"Hard work is good for the soul," Hamish said, materializing from the storage room with one of the large containers used to transport desserts to Castleglen. An eyebrow raised, he glanced from Laura to the clock she'd been studying. "You know, my Castleglen delivery will take me right past the high school. I have a sudden urge to pay some of my former colleagues a visit and perhaps happen by the athletic field to watch the kids practice."

Laura's shoulders immediately loosened and she shot him a wry smile. "You and I both know that the high school is out of your way. But if you want to take the scenic route, I'd be grateful."

After Hamish left with the tortes for Castleglen, Carol entered with a cleaning rag and bucket in her hands. "The front is clean. I'm heading home now."

"See you tomorrow," Laura said, distracted by swirling concerns about the pranks.

Carol emptied the bucket in the sink. "Harvey once did a series on bullying when he was working as an investigative journalist," she said, as if she could read Laura's mind. "I understand how being on the receiving end of a lot of bullying might compel a victim to fight back."

Laura nodded. Carol was likely thinking of Brendan. He certainly seemed to have a strong motive and, aside from the attack on the quarterback, had means and opportunity. However, he simply didn't seem like the retaliatory type.

Marcus Parish, on the other hand, had behaved like a big bully at the game. Granted, it was difficult to imagine he'd inspire the loyalty of anyone on his former team to do his dirty work.

"Do you think Harvey could research Marcus Parish's history?" Laura asked. "Maybe he can find out where he was before he came to Loch Mallaig and why he left."

"I'm sure he'd be happy to do that," Carol said. "Especially if it gets him out of chicken duty tonight."

Feeling a little more at ease with the knowledge that at least *something* was being done, Laura mixed several batches of dough and stored them in the refrigerator before heading home to start supper.

When Henry arrived, Laura was dishing up their meal. Henry dropped his dirty uniform in the laundry room and unloaded his books on the side counter.

"How was practice?" Laura asked.

"Good."

"No problems?"

"Nope." He helped himself to a glass of milk and carried his plate to the table.

Laura picked at her own meal. Every attempt at initiating a discussion was met by a one-word response, usually delivered from a mouth full of food.

Henry finished in record time—even for him—and then surged to his feet. "Thanks for supper." He took his dishes to the dishwasher. "I've got homework."

"Okay." Laura began to gather up the leftovers and put them in the fridge. Was Henry upset about something or just being a typical monosyllabic teenager? She didn't have enough experience to know the difference.

She wandered aimlessly about the house, now regretting her decision not to attend the evening's Fair Knitting Ladies meeting. She slumped into her easy chair and pulled out the slippers she was knitting. Less than ten minutes later, after mixing up her knits and purls twice in the first row, she decided her mind was too preoccupied to concentrate on knitting.

She made herself a mug of hot cocoa and settled back into her chair with a new novel instead. Her cell phone rang. She glanced at the screen and, seeing Hamish's name, quickly answered it. "Do you have news?"

Hamish chuckled. "Might be. I didn't see any mischief, but Mr. Nelson, the track-and-field coach, sure is *carnaptious*."

"Translation?" Hamish often peppered his conversations with Scottish words, but this was another new one to her.

"Looking for a fight."

"Ah. Yes, I saw him have it out with Coach Bassett outside the locker room right after the itching powder incident. He was upset that the new football jerseys cost him a pole vault pit."

"Aye," Hamish said. "Might be motive to stop the football team's advancement to the finals. And he'd have access to the equipment."

"He told Bassett he wouldn't jeopardize the chances of a school team going to State, though," Laura said. "I think I believe him. The prestige of any of their teams being that successful is bound to boost the status of the entire athletic department."

"Aye. I suppose so." Hamish sounded disappointed.

Laura thanked him for keeping an eye on the situation for her, then headed to bed. Although she slept well, she awoke with the same concerns in her mind that she'd had the day before—and now she had the added stress of worrying about that evening's playoff game.

The first thing that brought a smile to her face all morning was discovering Trent sitting on the front porch of the bakehouse when she arrived.

She parked on the street and trotted up the walkway, laughing. "You must be desperate for a carb fix. We don't open for another two hours."

He shrugged. "I'm not worried. I have an in with the baker."

At his wink, her heart skipped. "Oh, you do, do you?"

He stood and reached for her hand, his eyes twinkling in the porch light. "I was hoping she'd agree to let me take her out to dinner tonight."

She longed to accept, but she already had important plans. "I can't. Henry has a big game."

Trent's frown matched her own. "But it's out of town, isn't it?"

"Yes, and I'm bringing snacks for the team." Laura brightened. "You're welcome to join me. I'd love it if you could."

Trent's shoulders drooped. "I can't leave my shop early. I have a group coming at five to pick up canoes and paddles they've rented for the weekend, and my part-timer asked for the night off so she can go to the game."

"Want to come to the game tomorrow night if they advance?"

Trent cringed. "Similar problem, different day. Who knew running an outfitter would be so time-consuming?"

"It shouldn't be this hard to make plans together," Laura said. "What about Sunday?"

"I'm free," Trent said, a smile returning to his handsome face. "How about a picnic?"

"And a hike afterward," Laura added.

"I like the sound of that."

"It's a date." Laura grinned. "Finally."

When Laura stopped to check the clock, she realized the entire morning had passed and she hadn't fretted over Henry's situation with the football team—no doubt thanks to Trent's surprise visit, which had put a much-needed spring in her step.

Carol bustled into the kitchen. "Hamish has volunteered to help me serve customers until closing," she announced. "You and Molly can take off with Bridget as soon as she gets here from her noon class. That way you'll be able to leave early enough to meet the team's bus."

"Are you sure? I feel bad enough leaving all the cleanup to you."

"Don't give it a second thought. I know you want to be there. Besides, you have a team to feed."

"Yes I do." Laura grinned, then realized that spending the morning not thinking about the football team had made her forget to ask Carol about the Fair Knitting Ladies meeting. "Did you get a chance to ask Pippa about her nephew last night?"

Carol shook her head. "She wasn't there. I'll try calling her today when the shop's quiet." She nodded toward the coolers lining the wall. "Bridget will be here soon. You'd better get those packed."

A couple hours later, Laura, Bridget, and Molly pulled into the parking lot of Houghton East High School, which was hosting the district finals even though their team wasn't participating.

"There's our opponent's bus," Molly said as she steered her Honda Fit into a space across the lot from a burgundy and black bus with a fierce grizzly bear graphic emblazoned on the side.

"Where's Loch Mallaig's bus?" Bridget asked.

Reflexively, Laura's stomach clenched. "They left fifteen minutes earlier than we did. They should have gotten here first."

Molly dismissed her concern with a cheerful wave. "They probably stopped to stretch their legs."

"I hope they didn't get a flat tire or something," Bridget said. Molly scowled at her and Bridget immediately became contrite. "Sorry. I'm sure they'll be here any minute."

Laura climbed out of the car and peered down the road. "I'm sure you're right." She hoped she sounded more optimistic than she felt. She slipped her hand into her jacket pocket and felt for her phone. Would Henry be embarrassed if she called to ask him what the holdup was? She decided not to risk it. "This gives us a chance to scope out the competition."

Molly shivered and zipped her parka up to her chin. "I don't envy those boys having to play in this chilly weather."

Bridget made a sympathetic face. "Or the cheerleaders in those short skirts."

"I'm sure they warm up once they get moving," Laura said. "It's only seat warmers like us that will feel the chill." She thought about unpacking the coolers from the trunk, then changed her mind. "We might as well leave the food here for now."

The stands were already filling with fans. Laura recognized many familiar faces from Loch Mallaig proudly dressed in the school's green and gold colors. However, the seats on the opposite side of the field were awash with burgundy and black. A cheer erupted from the opposing crowd as several Grand Hollow Grizzlies players ran on the field and began doing drills.

"At this rate, our guys won't get a chance to warm up," Laura fretted.

"Isn't that Marcus Parish?" Bridget pointed to a clutch of men, some in referee uniforms, standing near a table on the sidelines. "What's he doing here? Didn't we squeeze out the Marauders with our win last week?"

"I thought so," Molly agreed. "But I'm not sure how the tournament works. Do you, Laura?"

"Not really, but maybe one of those guys has heard from our coach." Laura edged toward the men with Bridget and Molly on her heels. She slowed as they got close enough to hear the men's conversation.

"I say if they don't make it by the scheduled start time, they forfeit the game," Coach Parish declared.

Laura clenched her hands. The man was infuriating.

"Let's not be hasty," said a kind-faced man wearing a burgundy jacket with the Grizzly logo embroidered on the back. "I'm sure if your team was delayed, you'd appreciate our extending a little grace."

Marcus grumbled something inaudible. Did he despise Loch Mallaig so much that he still wanted them to fail? Laura yanked her phone from her pocket and called Henry.

He picked up on the first ring. "We ran out of gas," he said the instant he answered.

She moved out of earshot of Parish. "Where are you? We'll bring you gas."

"We're already at a gas station," Henry said, but he didn't sound relieved. "There's a leak in the fuel line and the bus driver refuses to drive on."

"What?" Laura shot a panicked glance at Molly and Bridget.

"Kit says it's bad karma," Henry said quietly. "What we get for picking on Brendan."

"How far away are you? There's got to be something we can do. Is another bus on its way?"

"Yeah, we're waiting for it. I'm sorry, Aunt Laura."

"For what? This isn't your fault." She eyed Parish once more, not liking how chummy he and the other coach seemed to be. They laughed as if sharing a private joke. "You have nothing to be sorry about."

"I do. I didn't want to say anything, but I thought you were wrong to worry." Henry's voice broke. "You were right, though. Someone really is out to get our team."

9

"Can I speak to your coach?" Laura asked Henry as she scanned the stands, now filled with anxious Loch Mallaig fans. Her heart stuttered when she spotted a familiar silver-haired figure ambling toward the bleachers. *It can't be.*

"Bassett here," Henry's coach said a moment later.

"Umm." Laura suddenly forgot why she was on the phone. The man she'd spotted shifted toward her. Definitely Kirk Donovan. *What's Dad doing here?* She scanned the vicinity for her mother, Marie.

"Hello?" the coach said impatiently.

Keeping Kirk in sight, Laura angled slightly away and cupped her hand around her phone, even though her dad was too far away to hear her conversation. "You should know Marcus Parish is here declaring we'll have to forfeit the game if the team doesn't arrive by the start time."

"Parish?" Bassett barked. "This has nothing to do with him."

"Be that as it may, he's pressuring your opponent's coach to claim the win." Laura's voice rose in pitch as her mom joined her dad and pointed Laura's way.

"Take it easy, Ms. Donovan. I've already spoken with the tournament organizers, and the Grizzlies coach has agreed to a half-hour delay. Granted, getting there in that time could still be tight."

"There are tons of people from Loch Mallaig already here with their own cars," Laura said. "I can round up volunteers to drive out and pick up you and the boys." She tapped Molly's arm and gestured to her parents. Her friend understood at once and went to stall them.

"I appreciate the offer, but there isn't time," Bassett said, "We are still at least twenty minutes away."

Laura groaned. She didn't need Carol's help to do the math. And to make matters worse, her parents had clearly made the trek here from Marquette to watch their grandson play. What was she going to tell them? Although surely if the coach could prove someone messed with the bus, the tournament organizers would have to give the team all the time they needed. "Henry said the gas line is leaking. Was it sabotaged?"

"I don't want to speculate," Bassett said. "I'm not a mechanic." In the background, a teen called for him. He sighed. "As one of my players is reminding me, another team's bus stopped at the same rest stop we did shortly before our driver noticed the gas level dropping."

"Parish's?" she asked, even though he appeared to be at the tournament on his own.

"No, the Grizzlies, the team granting us the game delay. But if their goal had been to shut us out of the tournament, they wouldn't be making the accommodation."

Acknowledging that it didn't make sense, Laura forced her shoulders to relax. It could just be a coincidence. She wished the coach luck and hung up.

"It's as if the team's jinxed," Bridget said, when Laura repeated what Bassett had told her.

"I'm afraid it's more sinister than that." Laura pasted on a smile for the benefit of her parents, now approaching with Molly.

"Look who I found," Molly said brightly.

"How did you get here?" Laura asked, feeling a sudden swell of guilt for not thinking of offering to drive them herself.

Kirk's eyes twinkled with amusement. "I may be teetering toward eighty, but I can still find the gas pedal on the old car. Forgot where the brake pedal is, though."

Marie playfully swatted his arm with the back of her hand. "Don't pay any attention to him, dear. Toby drove us."

Laura scanned the faces nearby. "Did he stay?" A former Air Force pilot turned private instructor who lived in Copper Harbor, Toby Griffin was a good friend of Brody's and like a brother to Laura.

Toby materialized at her side and slung an arm around her shoulders. "Of course I stayed. I couldn't miss Henry's game." His sandy-blond hair still sported a crew cut with no telltale gray in sight.

"Let alone the chance to taunt Brody with the fact." Marie smiled at him.

Toby grinned shamelessly right back at her. "You know me too well, Mrs. Donovan." He glanced pointedly around. "So where is Henry? And his team for that matter? We didn't see their bus in the parking lot."

Her father checked his watch. "We thought we were going to miss the kickoff."

"The bus had some mechanical trouble," Molly explained. "Don't worry—their opponent's coach is being understanding."

Laura squirmed. She hated keeping secrets from her parents. Not that she knew for certain that someone had tampered with the bus's gas line, but it seemed likely, given everything else that had happened—which she also didn't want to worry her parents about.

"As he should," Marie said with the kind of starch in her voice Laura recalled from her youth. "Shall we stake out our seats while there are still good ones to be had? They've got a great turnout."

As they skirted the field to get to the bleachers designated for Loons fans, the Grizzlies coach waved his practicing players in and motioned them toward the school. Before he could follow them inside, one of the refs stopped him. "How long are you willing to delay the game?"

"As long as it takes," the coach said with a shrug.

The ref blinked, apparently surprised by the answer.

Frankly, so was Laura. Granted, winning a game by forfeit wasn't the same as actually playing it, but it would get them to tomorrow's final—and wasn't that what they wanted?

"College scouts are here," the Grizzlies coach added. "Tonight's game could be more important to my best players than tomorrow's finals."

"Did you hear that?" Molly asked Laura.

"Brody did mention that college scouts often come out to the bigger tournaments," she answered.

"Has Henry talked about it?" Marie asked.

Laura shrugged. "Nothing specific, though I know he'd love to play in college."

While Toby and the elder Donovans went ahead, Bridget caught Laura's and Molly's arms and held them back. "This could be why someone nicked the bus's gas line," she whispered. "To frazzle our team so they don't play as well as they can. It would make the other players more impressive to the scouts. Don't you think?"

"It's possible," Molly said.

Laura frowned, her gaze fixed on her parents getting settled in front-row seats on the forty-yard line. They deserved to see their grandson play at his best. If only she'd convoyed with the team's bus, perhaps they could have averted the whole mishap.

Toby backtracked and rejoined Laura. "Okay, want to tell me what's really going on?"

"What do you mean?" Laura asked, although the wobble in her voice gave her away.

Toby chuckled. "You've always been a terrible liar."

Instead of arguing, Laura gave Toby the abbreviated version of what was going on with Henry's team.

"But you don't know for a fact that someone is out to sabotage the team?" he clarified when she'd finished.

"It's pretty obvious," she said. "The quarterback was attacked. The team's uniforms were coated with itching powder. The practice equipment failed."

"The equipment failure could have been an accident," Toby reasoned.

"*Could* have been," Laura echoed.

"And you don't *know* that the attack on the quarterback is connected at all to the prank on the team's uniforms," he went on. "It could have been someone who didn't like him personally. From my experience, jocks can rub people the wrong way when they're a little too full of themselves."

"Maybe," Laura admitted. "Still, it's a little too coincidental that all these things should suddenly happen to the team, and during the tournament. Don't you think?"

Toby shrugged. "My girlfriend says the same thing when a bunch of incidences support my latest horoscope. And you know I don't believe in those. People see what they want to see."

Grimacing, Laura crossed her arms over her chest. "So you're saying I've been worrying for nothing for the past week?"

"I hope you have," he said. "Worrying doesn't help anything." Compassion seeped into his expression. "On the other hand, it doesn't hurt to be vigilant, especially where Henry's safety is concerned."

"Agreed," Laura said.

Toby asked where the bus was broken down, then gestured toward Kirk and Marie. "You go sit with your folks and I'll drive out and assess the bus's gas line. It shouldn't take long to determine whether or not it simply wore down or had a little help."

"At this point, I'm not sure you could get to it before it's towed away," Molly put in.

Toby shook his head. "I suspect it'll be a while before a tow truck gets there. You need a heavy-duty truck to pull a bus, and it might be hard to find one with a driver available on a Friday night."

"I'd feel better knowing for sure one way or the other," Laura admitted.

"It's settled then," Toby said. "Let your parents know I'm taking advantage of the game delay to run an errand in the area. I might not get back in time for kickoff, but I'll be back before halftime for sure."

"Thanks, Toby," Laura said. As he started to leave, another thought gripped her. "You won't mention any of this to Brody, will you? I don't want to worry him."

Toby winked. "Got it."

"He seems like a really nice guy," Bridget said as they continued toward the bleachers. "Did you two ever date?"

Laura barked a laugh. "No way. I knew him before he grew into a really nice guy."

Molly chuckled. "I can relate. My brother's friends used to drive me crazy when we were in high school. Though not as crazy as Graham did."

"Makes me glad I'm an only child, I guess," Bridget put in.

Just as they reached the stairs to where Kirk and Marie were saving seats, Molly caught Laura's arm. "Hey, there's that substitute teacher who's sweet on Officer Murdoch." Molly pointed to the far end of the bleachers, where Beth Templeton was speaking to a group of girls wearing Grizzlies jackets.

"We should ask her if Murdoch is coming," Laura said. "If he is, maybe he could stop on his way and examine the bus too." She signaled to her parents that they'd be a few more minutes, then led Molly and Bridget toward Beth.

Noticing the women approaching her, Beth said something to the girls and they walked off.

"Cavorting with the enemy?" Bridget teased as they drew closer.

Beth blushed. "They were students from a class I taught for a few weeks last semester."

"She's just kidding," Molly reassured her.

"Do you know if Officer Murdoch is coming tonight?" Laura asked.

"He isn't," Beth said, although she seemed pleased that Laura had assumed she would know. "He went out of town for his grandmother's birthday this weekend."

Laura couldn't hide her disappointment. "Oh."

Beth tilted her head. "What's wrong? Has there been another prank?"

"We're not sure. The gas line on our team's bus sprang a leak on the way here. That's why they're late," Laura explained.

"And it seems like a fishy coincidence," Molly added.

"I'll say," Beth agreed. "Not to mention dangerous."

Laura winced, not wanting to think about what could have happened.

Someone called to Beth from the top of the bleachers, so she excused herself.

"What do we do now?" Bridget asked.

Laura sighed. "Not much to do but wait to hear what Toby finds."

"We should watch for suspicious behavior," Molly said.

"We've got to be missing something," Bridget said. "A clue we don't realize is a clue."

"Maybe assuming one person is behind all the incidents is our first mistake," Molly suggested.

"If one person isn't, then the sudden surge in bad luck, or whatever you want to call it, is awfully coincidental," Laura pointed out. "And despite what Toby said about our take on it all, my gut tells me they are connected, deliberate, and malicious."

Laura peered across the field to where Marcus Parish was chatting with a man in a Michigan State ball cap. A college scout? Parish was the one person for whom she could tick all the boxes. He would know how to access the Loons' equipment. He had lived in Loch Mallaig long enough to know where he might find the quarterback after a game. He'd been at the game with the itching powder. And he was here today even though his team wasn't playing.

What if he'd made an extra stop on the way here—at the rest area where the Loons' bus had sprung a gas leak?

10

A cheer rose from the crowd when the Loch Mallaig Loons finally ran onto the field and completed a lap before lining up for the national anthem. A yellow school bus had been dispatched from a local elementary school and picked them up where their team bus had broken down.

"There's our boy!" Marie pointed to Henry, his helmet under his arm. "Go Henry!" she shouted, waving animatedly.

Henry glanced over and grinned at them.

The refs wasted no time in starting the game. From the first play, Laura wasn't sure if she liked being so close to the action. She soon found herself cringing over every clash.

Her mother showed no such qualms. The first time their quarterback snapped the ball to Henry, Marie surged to her feet. "Run, run!" To his fellow players, she yelled, "Take down number five, number seven!" When the Grizzlies' linebacker took down her grandson instead, Marie shouted encouragement to Henry between hissing to Kirk about the other Loons not protecting him well enough.

Amusement dancing in her eyes, Molly nudged Laura. "I had no idea your mother was so excited about football."

"Neither did I." Laura suspected it was more that Marie was excited about her grandson.

Laura scanned the area for Toby. She might be able to settle down and enjoy the game better if she at least had good news from him on what had really happened with the bus. Seeing no sign of him yet, Laura watched the sidelines for suspicious behavior.

Control of the ball soon reverted to their opponents. On the second down, a Loch Mallaig Loon tackled the Grizzlies' running back right in front of their seats. Laura was certain she heard a bone crack, but the ambushed player sprang up from the ground and trotted back to the line of scrimmage appearing none the worse for wear. Laura shuddered, thankful that at least it hadn't been Henry.

"Where did Toby say he was going?" Marie asked when he still hadn't returned by the start of the second quarter.

"He had an errand," Laura hedged. "I'm sure he won't be long now."

"Did you see that?" Bridget asked, remarking on a player's sneaky pass.

"I missed it," Laura admitted. Her head was on a swivel between watching for Toby and for potential saboteurs. Whenever anyone moved from their seat or among the players on the sidelines, she watched them carefully for any sign they were up to mischief. By the middle of the second quarter, Laura's legs started to hurt, and she realized that in her concentration, she'd been clutching her thighs, with her fingers digging in hard.

The cheerleaders did a series of cheers to perk up the crowd while players changed places on the field. Brendan quietly supplied the retiring players with fresh cups of water. No one seemed to be giving him a hard time today. *Too focused on winning the game, no doubt.*

Then Laura noticed his sister, Tina, watching him from her seat nearby. Her presence surprised Laura after how clear she'd made it at the bakehouse that football players repulsed her. Was she concerned enough about her brother's welfare to sabotage the team? Laura immediately nixed the idea that she might have cut the bus's gas line and risked her brother's safety.

But what if Tina was secretly concerned her brother was the one sabotaging the team?

Larry the Loon sidestepped along the entire stretch of the crowd, circling his wings to urge the crowd into a cheer. A pair of burly teens wearing Grizzlies gear called out insults.

"Nice legs, Duck Man," one taunted, but Kit ignored it.

Laura imagined Kit was used to the jibes from the opponents' fans. It came with the territory, and a willingness to dress up in a loon costume showed innate confidence.

The Loch Mallaig Loons intercepted the Grizzlies' pass and regained control of the ball. As the clock ticked down, the Loons quickly moved the ball toward the end zone.

The players lined up for the final play of the first half, and Kit dashed in front of the crowd once more, rousing a deafening cheer. The QB caught the ball, faked a throw to the wide receiver, then quietly passed the ball to Henry.

Laura surged to her feet. "Go, Henry, go!"

The Loons' offensive linemen plowed down their opponents like battering rams, clearing a path for Henry to run the ball to the end zone. A burly linebacker lunged for him, but Henry dodged his grasp and surged into the end zone. The crowd roared, and Henry treated them to a celebratory dance.

With whoops and high fives, his teammates surrounded him. Beside Laura, Marie jumped up and down, then Laura realized she was too. She grinned at her mom and gave her a big hug.

Molly tapped Laura's shoulder. "We'd better go grab the coolers from the car. These boys are going to need a snack."

"Oh, right. I got caught up in the excitement." Laura let out a giddy squeal. "Henry scored a touchdown."

"That will get the college scouts' attention," Kirk said proudly.

A shiver of excitement skittered up Laura's spine. "He's going to be so pumped. We'll be back soon," she said to her parents. "Bread on Arrival is supplying the team with their halftime snacks."

"We'll keep your seats warm," Marie promised, although between worrying about what else might happen to the team and cheering them on, Laura had scarcely noticed how chilly the air had gotten.

Bridget, Laura, and Molly quickly delivered the coolers and bakehouse boxes to the team's locker room. Brendan met them at the door and took everything inside.

"Three cheers for my aunt Laura!" Henry shouted from a bench just inside the door, and his fellow players obliged.

Laura's cheeks heated. "Enjoy," she said to the team, "and keep up the great playing!"

Coach Bassett joined them outside the locker room, letting the door close behind him. "I appreciate you ladies supplying the team with snacks," he said. "They're sure earning them today."

"Did you figure out what caused the bus's gas line to leak?" Laura asked, suspecting he had been on his way in the replacement bus by the time Toby arrived to assess the situation.

"No," he replied. "But don't worry. I doubt someone is out to get our team. We've had a rash of bad luck is all."

Bad luck. Laura wasn't surprised that an athlete or coach would perceive it that way. "Coach Parish being here is a little suspicious, don't you think?" she pressed.

Grimacing, Bassett tugged off his ball cap and raked his fingers through his hair. "Nah. The fourth-place team in the division had to back out of the tournament, which puts Parish's team in. They'll play the third-place team tomorrow morning, and the winner of that game will play the winner of this one in the final. So, I have no doubt he's watching this game carefully to study his potential opponents' playbooks."

"Why did the other team back out?" Bridget asked.

"Half the team came down with the flu." The coach slapped his ball cap back on his head. "Now *that's* serious bad luck."

If it was *the flu.* Laura met Molly's gaze and suspected she'd had the same thought. "For rivals, Parish and the Grizzlies' coach seemed awfully chummy," Laura said.

That news seemed to give Coach Bassett pause. A muscle in his cheek twitched. "I have faith in Coach Caldwell's character. He wouldn't do Parish's bidding."

Laura nodded, but she could come up with plenty of reasons someone might act out of character. Maybe Parish had something on Caldwell and had blackmailed him into damaging Loch Mallaig's gas line. A rush of guilt could have instigated his magnanimous offer to not demand they forfeit the game.

"I think it's better to err on the side of caution and stay on your guard," Laura told the coach. "I can understand why you'd shrug off the itching powder incident as a schoolyard prank, but the attack on your QB and the damaged training equipment, not to mention the possibility that your team's bus was deliberately compromised, are serious offenses. Any one of them could've resulted in a player being badly injured."

"What attack on my QB?" Barely contained fury lined Bassett's voice. "No one told me about this."

"It happened the week before last, after a game, I believe," Laura said.

"Henry told me about it," Bridget put in.

Bassett stormed into the locker room. "Johnson, get over here. You too, Donovan. Johnson, what's this Donovan says about you being attacked?"

The door shut, cutting off the conversation. Laura and her friends headed to the bleachers, but Toby intercepted them.

"You're back," Laura said.

"You missed Henry's touchdown," Molly added.

Toby grinned. "Actually, I didn't. I was walking to the bleachers when it happened and caught a great pic of it on my cell phone. I've already sent it to Brody."

"Great," Laura said.

"Then I spotted you guys heading to the parking lot and figured you were searching for me," Toby continued. "I couldn't catch up to you before you went inside, so I waited here to talk to you before we rejoined Kirk and Marie."

Laura's eyes narrowed, wondering if he had bad news. "What did you find out?"

Toby sighed. "The tow truck driver let me check out the undercarriage after he hoisted the front end, and I'm afraid you were right." He took a deep breath and met Laura's eyes. "The gas line looked like it was sabotaged."

11

Laura gaped at Toby. "Are you serious?"

Toby nodded. "I think this ought to be reported to the police."

"We can tell the officer from Loch Mallaig who's been investigating the other incidents," Molly said, "but unfortunately he's not around this weekend."

"Then we might want to get the local police involved," Toby said. "Without knowing the guy's motive, it's anybody's guess whether he'll act again—and how dangerous the next 'prank' is going to be."

Laura's shoulders tensed. "Now you're really scaring me."

Toby gritted his teeth. "Those kids are lucky diesel fuel has such a low vapor pressure, or a spark might have caused it to ignite. And I don't need to tell you how serious that would have been."

Laura's heart thundered.

"We could ask Beth Templeton if she has Officer Murdoch's number," Bridget suggested. "I'm sure he'll come straight here if we tell him about this. His grandmother would understand."

Bridget volunteered to track down Beth in the upper bleachers and ask for the phone number. The rest of them rejoined Laura's parents as the players trotted back onto the field, sparing Toby from explaining his absence in any detail.

Minutes into the quarter, Bridget squeezed into a spot between Laura and Molly. "Beth's calling Murdoch now."

"You didn't get his number?" Laura asked. She would have preferred to talk to him herself.

"No," Bridget whispered. "I figured you wouldn't be able to talk to him with your parents sitting beside you."

Toby, now sitting on the other side of her dad, caught Laura's eye and mouthed, "Try to enjoy the game."

Easier said than done. Laura sighed and refocused on the field. As the game progressed, she found her gaze straying to Henry more than ever, while he seemed to be studiously avoiding looking in her direction. Was he miffed that she'd spoken to his coach about the attack on Jason Johnson? Bassett hadn't exactly been subtle, and Henry might blame Laura for being dragged into the drama.

At the end of the third quarter, a brunette in a Loons jacket wandered over to the team's bench and Henry spoke to her. She shifted to talk to him, and Laura recognized Amy, the ex-girlfriend of one of the Loons' linebackers.

One of the players gave the girl a frown, then moved to the other end of the bench. Was he the player who'd dumped her? Could she still be angry enough with him to take revenge on the entire team? If so, though, why was she fraternizing with Henry?

Henry nudged Amy's arm and laughed. The girl's smile widened, her eyes bright.

"That's the girl Henry was with outside the movie theater the other night," Molly said. "She's the one whose honor he was trying to defend from the guy who punched him."

"Interesting," Laura murmured, a disturbing thought flitting into her mind.

Although there was no way Henry would sabotage his own team, what if Amy thought all football players were ultimately alike? Plus, she was on the track-and-field team, and according to Coach Nelson, they had been robbed of funding that was given to the football team instead. What if she was merely using Henry to get close enough to the team to exact her revenge?

Unsettled by the continued uncertainty surrounding the team, Laura had a hard time concentrating on their actual playing. Before she knew it, though, they had won handily and she was joining her parents and friends on the field to congratulate Henry.

"I'm so glad you were here," Henry said to Marie and Kirk after giving both big hugs. "Can you come to tomorrow night's game too?"

"I'm sorry, but we can't," Kirk said, regret clear in his voice.

"We're celebrating our friends' fiftieth anniversary," Marie explained. "We were in their wedding party. Otherwise, we'd be there in a heartbeat."

"That's okay. I understand." Henry gave his grandmother another hug.

Toby patted Henry heartily on the back. "Good game," he said. "I sent your dad a picture of your first touchdown. He's so jealous I got to be here when he couldn't."

Laura stepped close for her hug. "The rest of us will be here to cheer you on tomorrow night."

"Along with half the town, I'm sure," Molly added.

"Coach has us booked at a motel close enough to walk to the field if we have to," Henry said. "Nothing's going to make us late for the next game."

Laura's heart thumped. *Never say never.*

Henry's teammates called to him as they headed for the locker rooms.

"Gotta go," Henry said, then gave his grandfather another hug. "Thanks for coming."

"Good luck tomorrow," Kirk said, giving the boy one last squeeze before releasing him.

Laura stiffened at the sight of Amy following Henry and the rest of the high school crowd. Was that a grease stain on the back of her jacket—the kind she might get from crawling under a bus?

Toby tapped Laura on the shoulder, making her jump.

Amy was now walking hand in hand with Henry, her head against his shoulder. Laura chastised herself. *I'm letting my imagination get the better of me. That girl is obviously smitten.* Even if Amy had contemplated taking revenge on the jerk who had dumped her, surely she wouldn't risk hurting Henry in the process.

Toby motioned Laura aside. "Did the officer your friend called make it here?"

Laura scanned the departing crowds. "I haven't seen him. We need to find Beth and ask her what he said."

"Bridget and I can do that while you walk your folks out," Molly volunteered. She said goodbye to the Donovans, then grabbed Bridget's arm and steered her away.

Laura went with her parents and Toby to the parking lot. Before Marie climbed into Toby's SUV, she opened her arms to Laura, who practically melted into the embrace. She reveled in the comfort for a few extra moments. She was never too old to need a hug from her mother. Not wanting to let on that anything was bothering her, though, she didn't linger too long.

"Sorry we can't stay for dinner, but I think we've kept Toby out past his bedtime," Kirk joked as he came around the car to hug Laura as well.

"You've got more energy than two of me," Toby said gamely. Once the Donovans were inside the car, he fixed his gaze on Laura. "Keep me posted on what you learn, and have that officer call me as soon as you talk to him. If there's anything else I can do, don't hesitate to ask."

"Thanks, Toby," Laura said. "I appreciate you keeping this quiet."

"No problem." He shot her a wry grin as he opened the driver's side door. "But if Brody hears about it, you're getting all the blame for the secrecy."

"Fair enough."

Toby started the car and pulled out of his space. He was steering out of sight when Molly and Bridget returned.

"Beth says she couldn't get ahold of Murdoch, but she'll make sure he hears about what happened," Molly reported.

"Did you get his number from her this time?" Laura asked.

Bridget produced a small piece of paper with a number scribbled on it. "Right here. Although I got the impression Beth *really* wanted to be the one to talk to him."

"I'm sure she appreciates any excuse to call him." Laura glanced from the nearly empty bleachers to the quickly departing cars. "I guess there's no urgency at this point. I hope he'll be here tomorrow, though."

"We should alert Coach Bassett about Toby's discovery so he'll be extra vigilant tonight," Molly suggested. "We need to collect our cooler from the locker room anyway."

When they reached the building, the team was pouring out the doors and racing for their substitute bus. The coaches exited last, towing their wheeled coolers.

"Good timing," the assistant coach said. "On behalf of the team, thank you."

"You're very welcome," Molly said. "And congratulations. We'll be back with more for tomorrow's game now that we know you'll be playing."

"Just bring the cooler to Brendan at the bench," Bassett said. "Let him lug them around. It's what he's here for."

"Will do," Laura said. "While I have you, Coach, there's something you should know." She filled him in on how the bus might have been sabotaged, but regretted the cloud that seemed to settle over the man, dampening his high spirits over the Loons' victory.

"Rest assured, we'll keep a close eye on the boys," the assistant coach said.

Laura drew in a deep breath but couldn't manage to exhale it. How could she entrust her nephew's well-being to two men who were outnumbered ten to one by exuberant teenagers, when some lunatic seemed determined to stop them from playing?

Molly must have sensed Laura's sudden inability to move. She took the cooler handle from Bassett and gave Laura a nudge. "We'd better get going. The boys need their supper."

Woodenly, Laura accompanied Molly and Bridget back to the car. All the way home they tried to reassure her Henry would be fine—and Laura did her best to believe it.

Saturday evening, Laura's spirits lifted the instant she spotted Henry among his hearty and healthy teammates practicing on the field.

"My brother is so jealous he can't be here," she told Molly as they—along with Fergus, Carol, and Bridget—wound their way to their seats for the final game of the division tournament.

"It's a good thing this game didn't start until late," Carol said, "or I might have been tempted to close the bakehouse early. Not that it would have hurt business much. Half the town is here to cheer on our boys. I hadn't expected so many to come to an away game."

"This is a big deal," Fergus said. "My dad brought me up as a huge football fan. When he heard our high school team might go all the way to State, he tried to convince my mom to delay heading down to Arizona for a month so they could be around to watch."

Bridget huddled deeper into her coat to ward off the November chill. "I don't blame her for vetoing the idea. I wouldn't mind being in Arizona right now."

Carol chuckled. "It isn't even that cold yet."

"Maybe not for the Upper Peninsula," Bridget protested. "But remember that I'm a transplant. Growing up in Seattle didn't prepare me for this level of cold."

They all chuckled.

"Did any college scouts talk to Henry after yesterday's game?" Carol asked Laura. "Bridget said he scored two of the three touchdowns."

"Not that I've heard," Laura said. "The scouts probably have to consult with the rest of their department before they actually make an offer to a player. I hope Henry wasn't expecting to get an offer on the spot. If he was, he'll probably be disappointed."

"I'm sure Karl explained to the team how the process works," Fergus said.

The warmed-up players left the field and cheerleaders dashed out to stir up the fans.

"Moira looks as if she's been crying," Molly observed.

Bridget scanned the crowd in the stands. "I hope Frank isn't here giving her a hard time again."

Laura's stomach dropped. *Or up to mischief.* She hadn't noticed him at the previous day's game, so the possibility he could have sabotaged the bus hadn't occurred to her. Given the motorcycle he rode, he struck her as the type that would know his way around a vehicle.

"Carol, did you get a chance to talk to Pippa about Frank?" she asked.

Carol shook her head. "She wasn't answering her phone yesterday."

Laura expelled a frustrated sigh. Despite the previous night's win, her fitful sleep had been peppered with dreams of villains greasing the football, holding out hockey sticks from the field's sideline to trip their players, and digging holes in the field to trap the Loons. In every one, the referees had completely ignored the shenanigans.

In the light of day, she'd managed to banish the worry from her mind—until she'd found out that Parish's team had won their morning game and would face the Loons again in tonight's playoff. The matchup added another layer to her apprehension.

She scanned the sidelines for any sign of mischief-makers, Frank in particular. As a former player, Frank might've been easily bribed by the likes of Marcus Parish to throw his ex-teammates off their game.

Before Laura left Loch Mallaig, it had crossed her mind more than once that she should call the number Beth had given for Officer Murdoch. She was hesitant to hassle Murdoch on his day off, though. Would he even take her concerns seriously?

Now she scanned the crowd, searching for Officer Murdoch and Beth Templeton. Not seeing them, she finally decided it was time to call him. The call went to a generic voice mailbox. Assuming he must be on the phone, she opted to text him rather than leave a message. *I hope you're going to be able to make it to the game. We're playing our archrivals again and I'm really worried.*

A reply came within moments. *Got to think positive.*

"Who's that?" Molly asked, peeking at the phone screen over Laura's shoulder.

"I texted Officer Murdoch," Laura explained.

Molly squeezed Laura's arm reassuringly. "Everything will be okay."

Laura nodded. "I know, but I'll feel better once Murdoch is here. Preferably in uniform to instill the fear of getting caught into whoever's behind this stuff. Of any day something is bound to happen to the team, today's the day."

"Now, now, you're supposed to be positive," Molly said.

"I am," Laura replied drily. "I'm positive something's going to happen."

A few moments later, Beth wandered past them, looking a little lost.

"Hey, Beth," Laura called. "Do you need a seat? We have room here." She scooted over and patted the empty spot between her and Molly.

"Will Officer Murdoch be joining you?" Laura scanned the direction from which Beth had come. "Or is he sticking close to the field?"

"Um." Beth frowned, appearing uncharacteristically ruffled. "I promised an old friend I'd sit with her." She motioned to the stands where most of their opponent's fans sat, then dropped her arm, her cheeks reddening. "I didn't know which side I should sit on. I substitute teach at both schools."

"Oh." Laura hadn't considered Beth's loyalties might be divided. "I didn't realize you were still teaching at the other school."

"I'm not," Beth said. "Not this semester anyway. I'm filling in for an English teacher who's on maternity leave, so I'm only at Loch Mallaig High. But today I was to catch up with a few friends I haven't seen in a while."

Molly clapped her hands. "Here come our boys!"

Appearing relieved for the diversion, Beth waved and hurried off without answering Laura's question about Murdoch and leaving her to wonder if Dalziel would be attending the game at all.

Loch Mallaig's fans surged to their feet and cheered their players running onto the field. At the sight of Henry's number eight jersey, Laura felt as if she might burst with pride. She snapped a picture of the field and another of the cheering crowd and texted them both to her brother with a short message. *Wish you were here.*

His reply was almost instantaneous. *Me too. Keep me posted on how it's going.*

Will do, Laura typed back, then pocketed her phone to sing the national anthem.

After the anthem, the Marauders won the coin toss and Laura searched the sidelines once more for Murdoch. Not seeing him, she sent a text. *The game's starting. Are you here yet?*

Ha, funny guy, came an immediate response.

Laura's heart sank. The text didn't sound like the man she knew. She tapped a reply. *Is this Officer Murdoch?*

Sorry, you have the wrong number.

Laura whipped out the small piece of paper from Beth. The ink was smudged, leaving the numbers a tad ambiguous. Was that a nine she'd mistaken for a seven? She showed the paper to Molly. "What would you say that number is?"

"A seven."

Laura frowned and scanned the rest of the number. "What about this one?" She pointed to what she'd assumed was a six but could have been a badly scribbled zero.

"A six," Molly concurred. "Why?"

"It wasn't Murdoch texting me back. So either I'm misreading the digits or Beth gave us the wrong number."

"I'm sure it wasn't deliberate," Molly said. "Try to enjoy the game. If Murdoch couldn't make it, I'm sure he would have asked another officer to come instead."

"You're right, of course. He's responsible that way." Laura pocketed her phone once more, then joined the Loch Mallaig fans in a rousing cheer.

The Marauders managed to make it to the twenty-yard line before the Loons gained control of the ball. They got it to their thirty-yard line before Parish's team reclaimed possession, and so it went for the first two quarters of the game, turnover after turnover but with neither team managing to score.

"My grandkids would be disappointed," Carol said when a time-out was called seconds before the halftime buzzer was due to sound. "They're only interested in the candy they get when our team scores a touchdown."

Everyone laughed, except Laura, who groaned instead. "If the game goes on like this much longer, I might get an ulcer."

"It is a nail-biter," Fergus agreed. "The teams are pretty evenly matched."

"To think, if the other team hadn't withdrawn from the tournament because of illness, this would be a whole different game," Bridget said. "We certainly wouldn't be playing Parish's team."

At the thought that Parish might have somehow infected half his rival team with the flu, Laura cringed.

Molly interrupted her thoughts. "Should we take the snacks over now?"

"Good idea," Laura agreed. "I think you and I can handle it."

Laura and Molly hustled to Laura's Beetle and brought back a large cooler and a few bakery boxes just as the players ended their huddle and ran onto the field for one of the final plays of the first half.

Brendan was rolling a fresh canteen of water toward the bench, but he was moving slowly and his face had a green tinge. "Coach, I don't feel so good. I'm going back inside."

Coach Bassett spared him an irritated glance, then shouted encouragement to his players. The down ended with two seconds still left on the clock. Bassett applauded his players' efforts, although there was no way they could score from this distance in the time remaining.

Of course, that didn't stop Larry the Loon from prancing sideways along the edge of the field, urging the fans into louder cheers. At the halftime buzzer, Bassett summoned Kit to the bench.

Kit removed his headgear. "What is it, Coach?"

"I need you to take over canteen duties," Bassett answered.

"But it's halftime and I'm part of the show. Where's Brendan?"

"Sick," the coach barked. "And do I need to remind you that if we can't keep our players hydrated, you'll have nothing to rouse the crowd about?"

"Yes, Coach." Kit set his loon head on the ground and began filling cups from the canteen.

"I don't like the sounds of this," Laura said to Molly. "Keep watch here for a minute. I'm going to talk to Brendan." She ran into the school and followed the signs to the locker rooms. One door had a sign on it indicating that it was reserved for Loch Mallaig's team. Instead of barging in, she nudged the door slightly open. "Brendan, it's Laura Donovan. Are you okay?"

A toilet flushed in response, followed by the sound of running water. A moment later, Brendan emerged into the hallway, a paper towel clutched in his hand. His face appeared slightly less green. In fact, his cheeks were now bright pink.

"You poor thing," Laura said sympathetically. "When did you start feeling sick?"

"I got a stomachache all of a sudden when I went back out to the field with the canteen," he answered weakly.

"What did you drink or eat before you felt sick?" Laura pressed, fears mounting that he might've been poisoned somehow.

"I haven't eaten anything since breakfast," Brendan said.

"What about drinks?"

He frowned and started to shake his head, then nodded. "Oh yeah, I had one after refilling the water cooler."

"From the canteen?"

"Yeah."

"Where did you fill it up?"

He pointed toward the locker room. "There's a special tap in there for filling large jugs and ice baths and stuff."

Laura decided there was no way Parish could have sabotaged it coming straight from the tap. "Did you leave the canteen unattended at any time?"

Brendan's eyes widened. "I forgot my hat inside. I left the canteen in the hallway so I could run back in for my hat before I went out to the field."

"And did you drink from it before or after that?"

He grabbed his middle, clearly attacked by another wave of illness.

"After," he mumbled and ran back into the locker room.

Fear shot through Laura as she sprinted back out to the field. When she arrived, Kit was handing out cups to the players, and the quarterback was lifting his to his lips.

"No!" she screamed. "Stop!"

12

"Don't drink the water!" Laura warned. She grabbed Coach Bassett's arm. "I think it's been tainted."

The QB spat out what was in his mouth.

"Brendan got sick after drinking the water." Laura searched the boys' faces until she found Henry. He didn't have a cup yet, thank goodness. She whirled and scanned the crowd for Amy, Frank, Marcus Parish—anyone connected to the previous pranks who could have been lurking near the locker room and could have tainted the canteen. She spotted Brendan's sister, Tina, in the crowd, but she wouldn't have pulled this stunt and risked her brother getting sick too, would she?

"Go inside, guys," Coach Bassett told his players. "Get a drink from the water fountain."

Kit tipped the water cooler over to pour the contents onto the ground. "I'll clean this out and get a fresh supply."

Laura waved her arms. "Stop," she ordered, and Kit quickly complied. "We need to take a sample. Bridget can test it to determine if something was added to it, and if so, what it was."

Coach Parish sauntered over. "What's all the hullabaloo about?" he asked, a smirk playing on his lips.

"You tell me," Bassett demanded.

Parish jerked back at the accusing tone. "Tell you what?"

"What did you put in my boys' water canteen?" Bassett snapped.

Parish snorted at the question's apparent absurdity. "Nothing."

"No? Then you won't object to taking a swig to prove to us it's safe to drink."

Parish balked. "You're telling me you think someone poisoned your water?"

"We don't know," Laura interjected. "But one of the kids got sick after drinking it."

"And," Bassett added, "you and your team are the ones who benefit from making our team sick."

Parish sobered. "If my boys are behind this, I promise I'll get to the bottom of it." He stomped back to his team.

Bassett slapped his ball cap onto the bench. "I can't believe this is happening." He pointed to the assistant coach. "Get into the locker room and make sure the boys are okay."

"Stop by the medic station on the way," Molly suggested. "Ask if they have anything you can give whoever drank from the canteen to help with those symptoms."

The assistant nodded and trotted off.

Parish jogged over from his side of the field. "My guys swear they didn't touch your water."

"Yeah?" Bassett said. "Will they put their stomachs where their mouths are and come drink it?"

Parish glared at Bassett for a moment, then he grabbed a cup from the stack on the end of the bench and filled it from what remained in the canteen. "Is this proof enough?" He saluted the other coach with the cup before gulping the contents. "I believe my boys." He crushed the empty cup. "The water tastes fine to me. I think you're paranoid, Karl."

"We'll see about that," Bassett said through gritted teeth.

Parish tugged on the brim of his ball cap. "You can't blame losing this game on me," he taunted before following his players into the school for their halftime break.

As the schools' marching bands took their places to entertain the fans, Laura drained the rest of the canteen into an empty water bottle for Bridget. "Maybe Marcus Parish has a cast-iron gut," she speculated to Molly.

"Or maybe it was the cup Brendan used that was tainted," Molly offered.

"I bet he threw it away." Laura screwed the cap on the bottle, then nodded to Kit to take the canteen away. Part of her wanted to suggest they hold on to the canteen to preserve any fingerprints. *If only Officer Murdoch was here.* Then again, he could be. Just because she'd gotten the phone number wrong didn't mean Beth hadn't convinced him to come. She scanned the area for the umpteenth time, but didn't see Murdoch or any other officer she recognized from Loch Mallaig. Should they involve the local police force? Since Parish hadn't reacted to the water he drank, any officer they told of their suspicions would probably think she was crazy. Or at the very least, wasting police time and resources over a *possible* prank.

After paying a visit to the locker room to see for herself that Henry and the rest of the players were fine and that Brendan was feeling better, Laura headed back to her seat.

"I phoned Greer while you were checking on Henry," Molly said. "She promised to ask Officer Murdoch if he's aware of what's been happening here and to find out if any of their officers are here watching the game."

Laura gave her friend a grateful smile. "Thank you."

"I wish I'd done it last night," Molly added glumly. "Perhaps we could have averted this crisis."

Laura nodded. "I feel bad for Brendan, but at least the players seem to have escaped unscathed."

Six minutes into the next quarter, a Loch Mallaig player broke through their opponent's defenses and scored the first touchdown of the game.

Carol rubbed her hands together. "Now things are getting interesting."

Bridget nudged Laura's arm and pointed toward the Marauders' bench. "Look at Parish."

The man was doubled over, clutching his stomach. He said something to his assistant coach, then dashed toward the school.

"He must be sick." Laura motioned to the water sample she'd given Bridget. "The water had to be tainted. And he drank a whole cup of it."

The Marauders' assistant coach flagged down the closest referee, and Coach Bassett joined them. A moment later, the ref called a time-out. During the lull, both teams' cheerleaders went into spirit-boosting routines.

"I'm going down there." Laura grabbed the water sample from the ground and stood. "Maybe Coach Bassett is finally ready to involve the authorities."

When Laura reached Loch Mallaig's bench, Bassett was grilling his players. Brendan sat on the bench, still a little pale but seemingly better. Kit, who had continued Brendan's water duties, hovered nearby.

"Who's seen Frank Aldridge?" Bassett barked. "It was bad enough to find out he jumped Johnson." He gestured to the quarterback, and Laura realized Jason must have admitted that Frank had been his attacker. "If he did this too, I'll have his head."

"I don't think he's here," Kit said softly. "I haven't seen him all weekend, and he usually doesn't miss a chance to make a crack about the loon costume."

Eyes narrowed, Bassett scanned the stands. "Then who's behind this?" His angry gaze met Laura's. "You don't think Parish would throw suspicion off himself by drinking that water, do you?"

Laura shrugged. "I don't know the man well enough to guess. I doubt anyone would willingly poison themselves, though."

Karl grumbled something under his breath, then asked, "Is Officer Murdoch here? I should have had him test the canteen lid for fingerprints."

"He's not," Laura answered. "I thought he was coming, but now I'm not sure he got my message."

"Any other Loch Mallaig officers here?"

"Not that I've seen, but Officer Anderson is trying to find out."

The ref summoned the players back to the field.

"I intend to speak to the police myself," Bassett told Laura. "Whoever is behind these pranks has gone too far this time."

Encouraged to hear that the coach finally intended to be proactive about stopping the incidents, Laura headed back to the stands. Beth Templeton intercepted her. "What's going on?" the teacher asked. "I saw the other team's coach run off."

"Why isn't Murdoch here?" Laura pulled out the crumpled slip of paper from her pocket. "This number you gave Bridget isn't his."

Beth emitted a frustrated sounding sigh. "I must have written it down wrong. I guess that explains why he hasn't responded to my voice mails. I'm sorry. I should've told you I never heard back from him. I was honestly hoping he'd turn up."

"Well, he didn't, and our prankster has struck again."

"Struck our opponents this time?" Beth's voice hitched. "How?"

Sensing there was more to Beth's stutter than a throat tickle, Laura studied the woman. It was natural she'd be surprised to think the other team had been targeted, but was there more to her surprise than that? Like maybe *she'd* slipped up somehow?

Laura racked her brain, straining to remember if she'd seen Beth leave the stands before the end of the first half.

"Ms. Donovan?" Beth pressed.

Laura shook the musing from her mind. "Sorry. We think the team's drinking water was tainted."

Beth's eyes widened. "Is Marcus going to be okay? Is anyone else sick?"

So, Coach Parish was Marcus now. Just how well did the substitute teacher know him? She'd said she taught at his school. Could she be Parish's mole at Loch Mallaig? On the other hand, if Beth was working with Parish to ensure their team won, why would she sweet-talk Murdoch into investigating the whole thing in the first place? Unless it was to ensure she remained above suspicion. *Hmm.*

Noticing Beth was waiting for her answer, Laura shook off the thoughts bombarding her. "Our equipment manager got sick first," she explained, "but he seems to be recovering."

"Why did our equipment manager drink the other team's water?" Beth asked, frowning.

"It was our canteen that was tainted," Laura corrected. "At least, that's what we think."

"Why did Parish drink our team's water?"

"To prove he didn't do anything to it. He claimed Bassett was being paranoid."

Beth blew out a breath. "Clearly someone did."

"Apparently."

Beth dug her cell phone out of her pocket, checked the screen, and put it away. "No word from Dalziel. He will be so disappointed he missed an opportunity to catch the culprit."

"You're probably right. Excuse me, I need to rejoin my friends." Laura returned to her seat and filled the others in on what had happened and her suspicions of Beth. "We need to keep an eye on her."

"If she's a substitute teacher, she wouldn't have had access to the sports equipment," Carol reasoned.

"She could have happened upon the storage closet when it was open," Laura argued. "Or tampered with the equipment when it was on the field."

"That would've been brazen." Disbelief colored Fergus's voice. "A lot of the school's windows face the field. Any number of people could have seen her."

"Good point," Laura admitted.

"Well, clearly someone is up to something," Molly said.

"And you don't think it was Frank?" Bridget asked.

"It seems not." Laura rubbed her hands against the chilly air. "He may have attacked Jason, but he hasn't been seen here all weekend. Of course, he could have followed the bus to the rest stop and snuck underneath to tamper with the gas line. If he's connected to the tainted water, though, he's either lying low or has an accomplice."

Bridget scrunched her nose. "He seems like the kind of guy who'd want to be around to gloat over the outcome of his shenanigans."

"Poisoning the boys' drinking water is hardly shenanigans," Carol said angrily. "It's criminal. Someone could have gotten dangerously ill."

"And we're no closer to figuring out who's behind it all." Laura sighed. Her cell phone chimed an alert and she glanced at the screen. "Brody is texting me. What am I going to tell him?"

"That we're in the third quarter and winning," Molly said firmly. "Don't worry him about the rest."

Laura did as Molly suggested, adding a happy face emoticon she didn't feel. Hopefully he'd interpret the brevity of her text as her being absorbed in the game. A moment later, Loch Mallaig scored a second touchdown. She *should* be happy. Henry was playing well, and despite everything, the team was on its way to a win.

The fourth quarter started with Loch Mallaig up by two touchdowns and still no sign of Parish.

"Parish has got to be regretting his cavalier behavior by now," Fergus said. "Not only is he sick, but his assistant coach doesn't seem to be up to the task of bringing home the win."

"This ought to make it pretty clear he didn't poison the water," Bridget added. "I doubt he'd bring such an illness on himself for any reason."

The fourth quarter felt as if it dragged on in ultraslow motion. Finally, the clock ran out and Loch Mallaig's fans surged to their feet in a celebratory cheer for the shutout game that won them the division title and guaranteed their advancement to the next level.

Carol gave Laura a warm hug. "Congratulations, Auntie. Your nephew made us proud."

A little of the tension that had been tightening its grip on Laura for the second half of the game eased and she found her smile. "He did play well, didn't he?"

"One day he'll probably be a star college player and we'll be able to say we knew him when," Fergus said encouragingly.

"It was a real nail-biter," Molly put in. "For several reasons."

"All's well that ends well," Carol said.

"And we have learned more about our saboteur," Molly said. "Like Bridget said, it seems unlikely it was Parish, not when drinking the water kept him out of the rest of the game."

Laura nodded. "And it wouldn't have been Brendan's sister, not with the risk her brother might drink the water too."

"So do you think it's Frank?" Bridget asked. "Maybe he got an accomplice to spike the water."

"It's possible, I suppose," Laura agreed.

"Or he's not connected to the attacks on the team at all," Fergus said. "Beyond beating up his rival, that is."

"That's the end of our suspect list, isn't it?" Bridget asked.

"No," Laura said. "Amy could be involved. We also wondered about Ben Merrells, but I doubt he'd jeopardize his team's chances of winning the tournament at this point. He might be second string, but he still gets to play."

"If his goal had been to play more," Molly put in, "he would have spiked Henry's cup alone."

Laura shuddered.

"Sorry." Molly squeezed Laura's arm. "I didn't mean to add to your worries."

"No, you're right," Laura said. "And I'm happy Henry wasn't targeted by himself."

"You know." Bridget tapped a finger on her chin. "If anyone in particular seems to have been targeted, it's Brendan, in a twisted sort of way."

Laura cocked her head, furrowing her brow. "How's that?"

"Well," Bridget mused, "the coach blamed him for the itching powder and the equipment failure. And if he hadn't gotten sick from drinking the water, guaranteed he would have been blamed for allowing it to be tainted, if not for doing it himself."

"Do you think he did?" Carol asked, a little breathless. "And then drank it to make himself sick so no one suspected him?"

Laura's chest tightened. He seemed like too nice a boy to be so devious. Sure, a lot of the guys teased him, but Brendan wouldn't put the team's victory in jeopardy just to exact revenge—would he?

After her run Sunday morning, Laura checked in on Henry in her spare bedroom for the second time. He was still sound asleep, catching up on his rest after the busyness of the past few days. She decided that if he didn't get up of his own accord at the sound of her shower or the smell of her making breakfast, she'd leave his food warming in the oven for him and slip out to church on her own.

An hour later, with no sign of Henry emerging from his room anytime soon, Laura wrote him a note and left. On her way down Yooper Boulevard toward town, she passed the Loch Mallaig Volunteer Fire Company's station. The fire truck out front made Laura think of the crumpled parking ticket she'd found in the football team's locker room, which had been issued for parking too close to a fire hydrant on Balmoral Lane.

Bridget's voice whispered in Laura's mind. *We've got to be missing something, a clue we don't realize was a clue.*

Could the ticket be the key to the mystery of who was targeting the Loons? Bridget had said as much at the time, then somehow they'd forgotten about it.

As Laura recalled, there had been no name on the ticket and part of the license plate number had been too smudged to make out, but maybe she should have shown it to Officer Murdoch. She wondered if Coach Bassett had talked to him yet about the weekend's incidents. Greer had told Molly he was still out of town, but that he was aware of what had happened at the tournament. Laura had no idea how the parking ticket could be connected, but she couldn't help feeling that it was integral to solving this mystery.

She decided she'd get the ticket from Bridget and give it to Murdoch first thing Monday morning. After all, the police must have copies of all the tickets they issued. He'd be able to find out to whose car it belonged.

Maybe something about seeing the place where the ticket had been issued would spark inspiration. She glanced at her watch and, deciding she had a few minutes to spare, drove past the turn for St. Andrews Church and continued to Balmoral Lane. Slowing to a crawl on the nearly deserted street, she looked for fire hydrants. There was only one—in front of the town library.

She sighed. Every student in the school would have a reason to go to the library. She paused at the curb and stared up at the two-story brick building. A library patron didn't fit her traditional image of a prankster.

Then again, maybe it was time to re-examine that image.

Suddenly brimming with questions, she drove around the block and parked outside St. Andrew's. As luck would have it, Grizela Duff, the town's formidable head librarian, and her husband, Ronald, were ambling toward the church's front door as Laura arrived.

Laura hurried to catch up to the full-figured woman with curly gray hair. "Grizela, could I have a word before you go in?"

The Duffs had a couple of their young grandsons with them. Grizela leaned down to them and said, "You laddies go off to your Sunday school class with your granddad. I'll catch up in a minute." Then, switching from kindly grandmother to strict librarian, she fixed her shrewd green eyes on Laura. "How may I help you?"

"Do you recall a high school student, or perhaps an adult searching the library for a book about how to make homemade itching powder?"

Grizela arched a skeptical brow. "I doubt we have any such book."

"Someone who might have done an Internet search then?"

"What's this about?" The Scottish native was using the same stern tone she usually reserved for hissing "*Haud yer wheest!*" at noisy library patrons.

"The Saturday before last, someone snuck homemade itching powder into the high school football team's jerseys. We haven't been able to ferret out who did it."

"What makes you think they got the idea at the library?" Grizela sounded deeply affronted by the assumption.

"I found a ticket in the team's locker room issued for parking in front of a fire hydrant on Balmoral Lane. The one hydrant on the street is in front of the library."

Grizela nodded. "Fair enough. I'm afraid I can't recall seeing a parking ticket being issued."

"I understand," Laura said. "It's a long shot that the parking ticket belongs to our prankster."

"I certainly don't approve of such tomfoolery, but youths will be youths."

"Normally I'd agree," Laura said, "but in this case, the tomfoolery has escalated to far more dangerous pranks."

"Oh dear. That is disconcerting. If you find out who the ticket belongs to, I might be able to help," Grizela offered. "I could at least share a list of which books he or she recently borrowed."

Laura resisted the temptation to ask her to search Amy's borrowing history. "I would appreciate that," she said instead. "Thank you."

The church bells chimed, and they both hurried inside. Grizela joined Ronald in their usual place. Spotting Carol and Harvey, Laura slipped into the pew beside them.

"Well, if it isn't the cat who caught the canary," Carol whispered. "Why so pleased with yourself?"

"I think I might have a lead," Laura said. Organ music started playing, so she patted Carol's arm. "I'll tell you about it later."

After a lovely service that included Reverend Stuart Findlay's sermon about the importance of loving thy neighbor, Laura and the MacCallans filed out of the sanctuary with the rest of the congregation.

In the foyer, Carol nudged Laura's arm. "There's Pippa. Let's go talk to her." Carol flagged down the slim redhead and, after exchanging pleasantries, asked about her weekend.

Pippa's eyes brightened. "Wonderful! We went to my in-laws' cottage Friday after school with the boys and my nephew Frank to pull in the boat and winterize the place. Came home last night. It was lovely. With the boys getting older, they rarely want to hang out with us like they used to. But this weekend, we worked together, hiked, and played games, just like old times."

"That sounds great." Laura smiled, hoping she sounded sincere. To be honest, she wasn't sure if she was relieved or not to hear that Frank had an alibi. If he was with Pippa's family all weekend, he couldn't have poisoned the water canteen, and it was unlikely he would have had time to sabotage the bus. Which crossed one more suspect off their list.

"I noticed a fair-haired lad hanging out with your nephew at one of the football practices last week," Laura said. "Do you know who he is?"

Pippa frowned. "Yes, Darren Jacobs. I can't say I've been impressed with Frank's behavior since he started hanging out with that boy."

"They're pretty tight, then?" Carol asked.

"They were," Pippa answered, "but my son said they had a falling-out Thursday night. That's why he asked if Frank could join us for the weekend. Why? Is Darren in some sort of trouble? It wouldn't surprise me."

"We're not sure," Laura said. "Frank and Darren weren't being very nice to the cheerleaders at football practice, and I wondered if they might be behind the pranks played on the team this weekend."

"Well, I can vouch for Frank." Pippa shrugged. "Can't speak for Darren, though. He's actually not in school, so I can't imagine what reason he'd have to prank the team. I'm not sure if he dropped out or if he's a year older than Frank and graduated last year. I heard he works part-time at the lumberyard."

"Thank you, Pippa," Laura said. "Please don't mention our asking to anyone. We don't want people to think ill of him for no good reason."

"I understand." Pippa mimicked zipping her lips.

After saying goodbye to Pippa, Laura and Carol caught up to Harvey outside the church. "Learn anything?" he asked.

"Frank has an alibi," Laura said. "We're still not sure about his friend, but we have a name for him now—Darren Jacobs. Although, unless Frank put him up to the pranks, he doesn't have any perceivable motive for going after the football team."

"He works at the lumberyard," Carol added.

Harvey's face grew thoughtful. "I'm fishing with the owner, Vince Commons, this afternoon. Maybe I could ask if Darren was working yesterday."

Carol beamed at her husband. "I knew I kept you around for a reason."

"Glad I can remind you of it from time to time," he answered with a wink, then turned back to Laura. "I also got some background on Marcus Parish."

"Anything useful?" Laura twisted her lips. "Not that we suspect him anymore, I guess."

"For what it's worth, I got the sense some people thought he was railroaded out of his coaching job at Loch Mallaig High because Bassett didn't get along with him." Harvey raised his eyebrows. "And Karl Bassett is a longtime friend of Principal Groves."

"Interesting." Laura motioned with her hand. "Go on."

"Parish was well-liked at his previous school," Harvey continued. "He was an assistant coach there, so moving to the head coach position at Loch Mallaig High was a step up he couldn't refuse. He was only here a couple of years before he got the job coaching the Marauders."

"He's obviously good at his job, given he brought his new school's team to the division finals his first year coaching them," Carol said.

Harvey nodded. "It's their first time getting that far too. People describe Marcus as even-tempered. He doesn't sound like the type to seek revenge against Loch Mallaig or to sabotage our team to advance his own."

"Did Carol tell you his team wouldn't have been in the division finals if the other team hadn't contracted the flu?" Laura asked.

"She did," Harvey confirmed. "I looked into it. There was a big outbreak at the school according to the paper. It wasn't the football players alone who were knocked out of commission."

"That puts my suspicions of Marcus Parish to rest, I suppose," Laura said.

"Laura, aren't you supposed to be meeting Trent for a picnic lunch?" Carol glanced at her watch. "It's already past noon."

Laura's stomach dropped. "Yikes! I forgot all about it. And I haven't made any food." She dug her phone out of her purse. "I had my phone silenced. He's probably been trying to reach me." Sure enough, there were three missed texts from him. "I've got to go."

Dashing to her car, she called Trent to apologize. After quietly listening to Laura give a recap of her weekend, Trent said calmly, "It's no problem."

Although she believed he was sincere, Laura couldn't help but feel a wave of guilt. "I'm sorry. This is not like me at all."

"I know," Trent reassured her. "Your concern for your nephew is natural. And I didn't expect you to prepare food. I ordered a couple of box lunches for us from Neeps and Tatties, and they'll be ready in twenty minutes. I'll pick them up, then swing by your place. Does that work?"

"Sounds perfect. See you soon." Laura rushed home to change before she left again. She found a note from Henry on the table saying he'd gone out with a friend and would be back by suppertime. She suspected "friend" was code for Amy. Laura hadn't asked him yet about the girl and wondered if she should.

Shaking her head, she decided it could wait. She had her own date to go on.

Monday morning, Laura stayed in the kitchen and focused on baking. Spending the previous afternoon with Trent had soothed her frayed nerves. She didn't want to waste another week feeling like a beach ball adrift on the lake, having her emotions tossed around by one wave of speculation after another.

Despite Laura's attempts to focus on the afterglow of her date, however, her conversation with Grizela flitted through her thoughts. She needed to check with Officer Murdoch about the recipient of the parking ticket, which Bridget was bringing to work with her later.

Molly slipped into the kitchen to collect another tray of biscuits for the display. "Do you need any help in here?"

"No thanks. I'm good." Laura swiped at an itch on her forehead with the back of her flour-covered hand. "Please let me know if Officer Murdoch comes in. I want to show him that parking ticket, and if he comes here, it would save me a trip to the station."

"Sure thing."

An hour later, Carol entered the kitchen. "Harvey got home from fishing after I was already in bed, but he just texted me that Vince Commons confirmed Darren Jacobs was at work Friday and Saturday."

"There goes that lead," Laura said, slightly dejected.

Carol smiled and waved the regional newspaper in her hands. "Maybe this will make you feel better. One of our customers left it behind. The school's win is highlighted on the front page, and the article even mentions Henry by name."

"How awesome." Laura wiped her hands clean and skimmed the article. She immediately frowned. "This isn't good."

"What do you mean it isn't good? I thought it was well written." Carol peered at the paper over Laura's shoulder.

"It mentions the purportedly poisoned water that put Marcus Parish out of commission for the last half of the game."

"Yes, but they don't suggest that it was our school's doing," Carol countered. "They make it clear that it was our water supply that had been tainted."

"We didn't tell my brother about what happened," Laura explained, her nerves fraying once again. "I didn't want him to worry. But what if he reads this? All these articles are posted online, and he's bound to hunt down every last one of them. He's a proud dad that way. Boy am I in for a lecture for keeping him out of the loop."

"Oh." Carol winced. "Well, it is what it is. Why should you have to worry alone?"

"Because I'm in a position to do something to protect Henry. Brody isn't."

Carol chuckled. "Thinking we can protect our children is a delusion."

Laura made a sour face. "Thanks for the pep talk."

"Any time."

Laura shooed Carol out of the kitchen and went back to rolling out dough. Then she spread on a layer of butter and went over the whole thing with the cinnamon sugar shaker.

Hamish wandered into the kitchen. "I finished the morning's deliveries. Is that cake for the retirement party at the bank ready to go?"

"It's all set. In the box on the cart in the cooler."

Hamish made no move to fetch it. Curious about what had captured his attention, Laura glanced up. He stared at her dough, his features twisted in confusion.

Laura set down the shaker. "What's wrong?"

"What are you making?" Hamish asked.

"Cinnamon rolls."

He arched a bushy eyebrow and scratched his head. "Do you always sprinkle salt inside?"

"Salt?" Laura's gaze dropped to the dough, and her heart dropped right along with it. There were no cinnamon specks amid the crystals of sugar. She tapped her finger to the crystals and touched it to her tongue. "It's salt," she said, dumbfounded.

"Aye. That's what I said."

She gaped at the shaker she'd grabbed. It was the large saltshaker she'd used when making soft pretzels for the football team. A groan escaped from her lips. "I can't believe I did that! What a waste."

"Don't be too hard on yourself, lass. You have a lot on your mind." Hamish went to the refrigerator to retrieve the cake and came back to find Laura still staring forlornly at the dough. "You know," he said, drawing out the words. "I spotted some Scottish cheddar in the cooler. Perhaps a spot of that and a bit of ham might be the solution to your problem."

Laura's mood brightened instantly. "That does sound good." She grinned at Hamish. "Have you ever thought about a career in culinary arts?"

He hitched his thumb over his shoulder. "I'll stick to delivering cakes for now."

Just as Laura was pulling the revamped rolls from the oven, Bridget arrived early for her shift and bustled into the kitchen. "Here's the parking ticket," she said, holding out the plastic bag with the yellow paper inside.

Laura tucked it in her pocket. "Thanks."

"And I have the results from the water test," Bridget announced. "You were right about the water being poisoned. It had aloin in it."

"I've never heard of that," Laura said.

"Neither had I. When I described the symptoms Brendan and the other team's coach had and our suspicions about the water to my professor, he said they sounded like aloin poisoning. He took a snipping of aloe vera from his office plant and showed me how to test for it."

"So it's from aloe vera plants?" Laura clarified. "I thought they were edible."

"They are if you eat the gel inside the leaves. Aloin is found in the sap of the leaf's rind, so you don't want to eat that part."

"Wouldn't they have tasted it if there was enough in the water to make them sick?"

"Probably, as it's quite bitter, but our perp simply added some other flavors to mask it," Bridget explained. "Apparently Brendan frequently added sports drink mix to the water to help replenish the boys' electrolytes, so they wouldn't have questioned that."

"So all we need to do now is find out which suspects had access to an aloe vera plant." Laura rolled her eyes. "I have two at home, and I'm single in a tiny cottage."

"Lots of people do." Bridget remained animated, clearly excited about her discovery. "To extract enough to poison a canteen full of water, the culprit would have had to tear apart several large plants.

I checked with the local florist on my way here. They have a couple of medium-sized plants in stock, but it's been a long time since they sold any."

"You need to tell Officer Murdoch," a woman's voice declared from the hallway.

Laura spun around to see Beth Templeton in the doorway. "You heard?"

"Yes," Beth said. "I was on my way to the restroom."

Laura noticed that she pointed to the door marked *Laddies* instead of *Lassies*, which Beth had already bypassed.

"You need to leave this in Officer Murdoch's capable hands," the teacher went on. "A bunch of overeager amateur sleuths asking too many questions will only tip off the culprit that he's got to hide his tracks better. You need to hand this information over to Officer Murdoch now."

As if mentioning his name made him materialize, Murdoch appeared behind Beth. "What information is that?"

Beth blushed and smiled at him. "Did you get my message about what happened at the tournament this weekend?"

"Yes," he said. "Thank you."

At Laura's raised eyebrow, Beth said, "Once I realized I had the wrong number for Officer Murdoch's cell phone, I left a message for him with the station."

"I've just come from talking to Karl Bassett about the situation," Murdoch said to Laura. "He said you took a sample of the water."

"Yes, Bridget tested it at the college." Laura gestured to Bridget, who explained the results.

Murdoch nodded thoughtfully. "Maybe we should sit down and review what else you know."

"We can use the office upstairs," Laura offered.

Bridget begged off to start her shift, so Laura led the way. She stiffened when Beth took it upon herself to follow but resisted the impulse to send her back down. Once in the bakehouse office, Laura motioned for them to sit in the two empty chairs in front of the desk, then settled into the one behind.

"Okay, Laura, tell me what you know," Officer Murdoch said.

As Laura recounted what they knew about the pranks and gave Murdoch her list of suspects, she couldn't help but notice Beth edging her chair closer to the young officer's. Suppressing an eye roll, Laura finished by sharing Frank Aldridge's alibi for the weekend.

"That's pretty tight," Murdoch agreed. "Jason isn't pressing charges against him for the assault, and Frank denies having anything to do with the equipment failure or itching powder. I'm not sure I believe him, but when it comes to the attacks on the team and their equipment, I'm inclined to think a single perp is behind them all."

"Definitely," Beth said, nodding as if she considered herself an authority on such matters.

Murdoch rose. "Thank you for the information, Laura. I'll take it from here."

"There was one more thing," Laura said. "I doubt it's connected." She hesitated, reluctant to mention the parking ticket in front of Beth, but not really sure why. The woman's presence was oddly unsettling.

As if Beth could read Laura's thoughts, she said, "I'd better hurry down and collect my things. I need to get back to the school."

Once she was gone, Laura gave the officer the ticket and a quick summary of the parking ticket.

He scanned it and nodded. "I can find out who the car belongs to, but I'm not sure what you hope it will prove."

"Neither am I," Laura admitted.

With little more to add, she walked him downstairs. In the hallway, he took an appreciative sniff, and his gaze traveled to the kitchen counter, where Laura had left the tray of ham and cheese rolls.

She grinned. "Would you like one? You can be my guinea pig."

"I won't say no to a new Laura Donovan creation," Murdoch said with a shy smile.

"Hamish actually gave me the idea for them." Laura put two rolls in a bag and handed it over. "Hopefully this gives you the energy you need to find our prankster."

"Yes ma'am."

She walked the officer to the café, where Beth happened to be collecting her coat and to-go coffee from a table. The substitute teacher trailed Officer Murdoch out of the bakehouse, and for some reason, the sight irritated Laura.

"Something about that woman is really starting to get on my nerves," Laura said to Molly and Carol at the front counter.

Molly chuckled. "You don't like being called an amateur sleuth?"

At Laura's confused expression, Carol explained, "Bridget gave us a play-by-play of your conversation." She waved a dismissive hand. "Don't pay any attention to Beth. She's just trying to stroke Murdoch's ego."

Laura couldn't shake her unsettled feeling, though. "She's got some ulterior motive," she said. "I'm just not sure it's as innocent as that."

14

After Officer Murdoch left the bakehouse, Laura felt more disconcerted and distracted than ever. Trying to bake when she felt like this was pointless.

She'd like nothing more than for Murdoch to nab the person endangering her nephew. However, she wasn't about to wait around for him to do it. She washed her hands and marched out to the front counter. She'd ask every customer who came in if they'd attended the weekend's game and if they'd seen any of their suspects—without referring to them as such, of course.

Nelly Blakely, mother of the school's head cheerleader, Moira, walked through the door with another woman in her midforties—the right age to have a child in high school.

"Hi, Nelly." Laura slipped around Carol at the counter to serve Nelly. "Were you at Saturday's game?"

"Of course. Go Loons!" Nelly said, her smile revealing perfect white teeth. Her daughter had inherited her good looks, sunny disposition, and Loch Mallaig team spirit. "Aren't our boys doing well? Moira is so excited."

Laura turned her attention to Nelly's friend. "I'm sorry. I don't think we've met. I'm Laura Donovan."

The raven-haired woman offered Laura a hand. "Evaline Curd."

"Her daughter, Jasmine, takes photos for the school yearbook and paper," Nelly added. "She captured that fantastic action shot of Henry they used in last week's write-up."

Laura's ears perked up. "I imagine your daughter took hundreds of photos this past weekend."

Evaline smiled proudly. "Yes. I saw them last night while she was sorting them on her computer. I missed the games because of work, but seeing the pictures made me feel as if I were there."

"Does your daughter photograph the fans too?" Laura asked.

"Oh yes." Evaline shot a sideways grin toward Nelly. "She has some wonderful candid shots. I don't know how the yearbook committee will whittle down their choices."

"I'd love to see them," Laura said. "I imagine you've both heard about the trouble the team's been having with a prankster?"

Both women nodded. "Terrible business," Nelly said. "I don't understand why anyone would want to spoil such a nice event that way."

Evaline snorted. "I can think of plenty of reasons. I had three students, all from different school sports teams, try to sell me poinsettias last week for a fundraiser. A track team member's animosity toward the football team was shocking. I wouldn't be surprised if one of them tried to stop the football team from winning to stem the bleed of funds from their own sports program."

"I never thought of that," Nelly said.

I have. Laura exchanged a glance with Carol.

A middle-aged woman behind them said, "I wouldn't put it past one of those sports dads either. You know the type. They're super competitive and don't think their child is getting enough time on the field, or they want to stake out a spot for him with the college scouts."

"Oh, I know what you mean," Nelly agreed. "There was a dad like that at my youngest son's baseball game. The kids are eight years old, for heaven's sake!"

"You can never start too young," the newcomer quipped drily.

"I haven't noticed any football parents acting that way," Laura chimed in. "Have you?"

"No, thank goodness," Nelly said.

"But Ned Stevens's dad is fanatical about track and field," the other woman put in. "He's determined his son will go places."

Evaline shook her head. "And my daughter says Ned isn't even all that keen to go away to college."

"Was Mr. Stevens at the football tournament this weekend?" Laura asked.

"Not that I saw," Nelly said. "I've never seen him at a game. It's not his sport."

"What can I get you, ladies?" Carol interrupted as three more customers entered and lined up behind the small group chatting with Laura.

Laura helped Carol serve the customers, repeating her questions to the new arrivals. By closing time, she'd confirmed that all their original suspects, minus Frank and the track-and-field coach, had been at Saturday's game. Some of the members of the track team, including Amy, had attended the game, but Ned Stevens wasn't among them.

As Laura flipped the sign on the door to *Closed*, Evaline bustled up the walk, waving to get her attention. Laura opened the door. "Did you leave something behind when you were here earlier?" She didn't notice any forgotten bags or packages around the bistro tables.

Evaline climbed the porch steps. "No, I got this from my daughter for you." She held out a flash drive. "It has the photos from the tournament on it, as well as the ones from the game before. She hopes it helps you figure out who's pulling these pranks."

"Wow, thank you. I appreciate it." Laura accepted the drive, then hustled back inside and shared the news with Carol and Molly. "The evidence we need might be on this flash drive."

"Are you going to give it to Murdoch?" Carol asked.

"Not before I get a chance to study the pictures." Laura checked the clock. "And I don't have time now if I want to go watch Henry's practice."

"Give it here." Molly held out her hand. "I'll make a copy for you. That way if Murdoch is at the practice, you can pass it on to him."

As Molly ran up to the office, Laura returned to the kitchen to restore order and remove her apron. A few minutes later, Molly joined her and handed over two flash drives. "You go on to the practice. Carol and I can finish cleaning up."

Laura thanked them both and quickly made the short drive to the high school. The parking lot by the football field was surprisingly full for late afternoon.

As she was climbing out of her Beetle, a man emerged from a nearby sedan with a *My kid is an honor student at Loch Mallaig High* bumper sticker. "Do you know what's going on?" she asked him, gesturing to the crowd of people already gathered on the grass.

"Parents want to know what the school's doing to keep our boys safe," he answered.

Laura trailed the man to the football field, where worried parents were demanding precautions be taken. Several of the players hovering on the fringe looked embarrassed.

"I'll be driving my son to the next away game myself," one father declared, and three others agreed.

"We should book our own hotel rooms and provide them with food and water we've monitored ourselves too," a petite woman proposed.

"Enough," Coach Bassett said. "All this talk is distracting the boys from practice. You are, of course, welcome to make your own transportation and accommodation arrangements, but your boys might have other ideas. Part of the camaraderie of the team is traveling together. You can rest assured we will take every precaution possible to ensure nothing bad happens."

The assistant coach began putting the boys through their drills, and Coach Bassett fielded more questions from a few stragglers who lingered longer than the other parents. Laura waited until they, too, had dispersed, then approached the coach herself.

"Did Officer Murdoch offer any insights into who the culprit might be?" she asked him.

Bassett shook his head. "Nope, but I'm not convinced—and neither is he—that Marcus Parish is innocent simply because he drank the water. He may have done it to save face once he realized we were on to him."

"If that's the case, then we've probably seen the last of the pranks now that his team is out of the running."

"Let's hope so. Excuse me." The coach clapped his hands and called his players into formation.

She took a seat in the bleachers, where a few other worried parents had also stationed themselves. A woman slid down the bench closer to her. "Thanks for raising the alarm about the danger our sons could be in," she said. "My neighbor told me you've been talking to customers about it."

Laura winced. Henry wasn't likely to be happy with her if he heard she was the person to thank for the sudden uprising among parents. However, she had to admit she was glad she was no longer alone in worrying. The more people watching for trouble, the less likely it was to visit.

She peered at the players on the field and caught Henry sneaking a pointed glance her way. Okay, maybe she didn't need to stick around today. There were enough parents here to play guard duty. And if she left now, she'd have time to study the photos from Evaline's daughter before Henry got home.

Officer Murdoch was in the parking lot chatting with Beth as Laura made her way to her car. Surprisingly, he was smiling at something she was saying, and he appeared more relaxed than usual in her presence. Perhaps Beth's flirtations were finally working.

As she greeted the pair, Laura retrieved the flash drive from her pocket. "I've got something for you, Officer." She handed over the stick, explaining how she'd come by the pictures. She didn't know what to make of Beth's miffed expression. Was she annoyed that she hadn't thought to ask the young photographer for her photographs?

"I've got the information you asked for too." Murdoch handed her a slip of paper. "The car owner's name and address."

Laura thanked him and waited until she climbed into her car before unfolding the paper. *Delphine Lancashire*. Laura searched her brain for a connection, then snapped her fingers when it came to her. This must be Brendan and Tina Lancashire's mom. Laura sped back to Bread on Arrival, hoping she could catch her friends before they finished cleaning up.

Carol's car was gone, but Molly was at the gate to the backyard with Angus on a leash when Laura parked and climbed out of her Beetle. Angus yipped in greeting, and Laura walked over to give him a few pets as she caught Molly up.

"You'll never believe whose car got the parking ticket," Laura said. Prompted by Molly's eager expression, she went on, "The equipment manager, Brendan's. Or at least his mom's, I assume. Same last name."

"So that pretty much confirms the parking ticket has nothing to do with the pranks," Molly said.

"Not necessarily," Laura countered. "Bassett isn't ready to cross Parish off his suspect list because he drank the water. Maybe we shouldn't have been so quick to cross off Brendan."

Molly frowned. "But surely he wouldn't have made himself sick with the water *before* anyone else drank it."

"He might have if he wanted to ensure this time the coach didn't harass him for the problem, for not being careful enough." Laura mentally reviewed everything they knew about the incidents. "You've got to admit that he had a strong motive and the most opportunity, but I'm not sure if he had the means. I want to go to the library and speak to Grizela, find out if he's been researching poisons."

Molly's lips twisted skeptically. "It wouldn't have been too smart for him to sign out a book of poisons under his own name."

"No, but kids often think they're being sneakier than they actually are. And you know what they say. The bad guy is often the person you least suspect."

"Like the butler."

"Exactly. And I'm afraid the quiet types like butlers and Brendan are precisely the kind who might plot an elaborate revenge scheme."

"Angus has had his walk, so give me a second to put him inside and I'll go with you." Molly led Angus toward the exterior staircase that went to her second-floor apartment.

In the library ten minutes later, Grizela brought up Brendan's borrowing history on the computer and peered at the screen. "Nothing about poisons," she said. "The last book he borrowed was three months ago, and it was about World War II history."

Laura sighed. "Do you recall him being in any other time between then and now?"

Grizela's gaze drifted to the ceiling as if she was searching her memory. "His mom has been in a few times. She favors romances. His sister was in recently too. She needed some book for a college project." Grizela tapped a few keys on her computer. "An etymology book."

Laura thanked Grizela for her help, then she and Molly left.

"So, can we officially cross Brendan off the suspect list?" Molly asked once they were outside.

"I suppose. I was so certain that the parking ticket had to be significant, though." Another thought occurred to Laura, and she grabbed Molly's arm. "Wait. I can't believe I didn't think to ask. We have to go back in."

Grizela peered at them over the top of her reading glasses as they stepped inside once more. "Back so soon?"

"There's one more thing I'm wondering if you can look up," Laura said. "Books of a specific subject that have been borrowed recently."

"Such as books about poisons or how to make itching powder?" Grizela smiled. "I already did, and while we have three books that might have the relevant information—one being a book for writers to use for research called *The Book of Poisons*—none have been borrowed in recent months. I also checked our reserve history on the library's public access computers. There's no record of Brendan using them. It's usually the older folks who do, since most young people have a computer at home these days."

Laura didn't know whether to be disappointed or relieved. It wasn't as if she wanted Brendan to be guilty. She simply wanted the culprit caught so the team would be safe.

That night, Henry was quiet at dinner. Maybe enough of his teammates were embarrassed by their own parents storming the practice that he didn't blame her for instigating it. Granted, the gathering might have been inspired by the newspaper article, not Laura grilling customers.

Laura's phone rang as they were finishing their meal, and her brother's name appeared on the screen. She answered. "Hi, Brody. Henry's right here. Do you want to talk to him?"

"No," Brody said, his tone tense. "I want to talk to you. What's going on? Why didn't you tell me someone poisoned the team's water canteen? What else has been going on that you haven't told me about?"

Laura held the phone away from her ear for the sake of her eardrum. Henry, who had clearly heard his father's strident tones, cringed. Laura mouthed, "Did you tell him?"

Her nephew shook his head and mouthed back, "Not me."

"Henry is fine," Laura said into the phone. "All the players are fine. We didn't want to worry you, or overshadow their accomplishments. Besides, we weren't even sure that's what made the equipment manager and opponent's coach sick until the test results came in this morning."

"You should have told me," Brody insisted. "I'm his father."

"Rest assured the police are investigating," Laura said, infusing as much confidence and reassurance into her voice as she could muster. "And I, along with most of the other parents, am taking extra precautions and remaining hyperalert to ensure nothing else happens."

Brody sighed heavily. "I know I can trust you to do your best. I just hate that I'm not there too."

"Henry knows you love him," Laura reassured her brother. "And if you were stateside, he wouldn't be here. He wouldn't have had this great opportunity to play on a winning team."

"Okay," Brody said. "Let me talk to him."

Laura handed Henry the phone and took their plates to the sink to wash. Henry chatted briefly with his dad, then picked up a towel and began drying pots.

As Laura drained the dishwater and cleaned the sink, she stared at the aloe vera plant next to it. Recalling that Amy had a head for science, she asked, "Is Amy fond of botany?"

"Amy?"

The edge in his tone made her regret asking. She hadn't really meant to voice the thought aloud. *In for a penny, in for a pound, I suppose.* "Yes, Amy. Your girlfriend."

"I don't know who you're talking about." He clanked the pot into the cupboard.

Angered by the bald-faced lie, Laura whirled to face him, her tone stern. "Don't lie to me, young man. I understand that you might not want to talk to me about your friend, and you can say as much.

But if I can't trust you to be honest with me, then this living arrangement isn't going to work."

Henry stood frozen, mouth open, for a moment, then clamped his jaw shut. He seemed to be thinking hard about what to say next. "She's not . . . I don't . . ." He stopped and took a deep breath, then said, "I *know* her. She didn't poison the water, if that's what you're getting at." Then he stormed off to his room and shut the door with a firm click.

Hey, at least he didn't slam it. Laura took a few deep breaths and thought about what Henry had said. He seemed so sure Amy was innocent. Laura only hoped he knew the girl as well as he thought he did.

Tuesday morning, Laura arrived at the bakery extra early. She couldn't afford another day like yesterday, full of mistakes and distractions. Molly and Carol counted on her to do her share.

Molly came down from her upstairs apartment. "I thought I heard you come in."

"Sorry." Laura grimaced. "Did I wake you?"

"No, I had to finish our Thanksgiving media blasts, so when I couldn't sleep, I decided to just get up and do them." Molly started the coffee maker. "I think I'll take Angus for a quick walk before I shower, then I'll come down and give you a hand."

"No rush. Carol will be here soon." Laura set aside her bread dough to rise, then started a batch of bannock.

While Molly was gone, Laura made a good dent into her morning's to-do list and Carol mixed two batches of cookies.

Carol was up to her wrists in her third batch of dough when the phone rang. "Can you get that? My hands are goopy."

Laura glanced at the clock. It was barely after six. "I wonder who's calling so early." Laura tucked the phone under her ear as she punched down the bread dough. "Bread on Arrival, how may I help you?"

"I'm so glad I reached you," a muffled female voice said. "I need a chocolate sheet cake for tomorrow morning at ten. It should say, 'Congratulations on Your Retirement.'"

"No problem. Would you like any particular colors?"

"It's for a man. Whatever colors you think are best. Maybe instead of roses in the corners, you could put golf or fishing gear."

"Is this for pickup or delivery?"

"I need it delivered." She gave Laura the address. "And I'll need five dozen boxes of mixed pastries."

Laura's heart stuttered. "You mean five dozen pastries?"

"No, five dozen boxes. You know, the size that fit about six pastries each. You can mix and match all you want as long as there is a variety."

"You want sixty boxes? Six-oh?" Laura verified. "By ten o'clock tomorrow morning?"

"That's right. Will that be a problem?"

Laura tamped down a wave of angst over the large order and its short deadline. "No, not at all. Our delivery man will be there by ten." She took the woman's name and number and verified the address one more time before thanking her and hanging up.

"Whew," she said to Carol. "It's a good thing I started early today. We have a massive order to fill for tomorrow." Starting a fresh piece of paper, Laura copied out the writing the client had requested for the cake and slid it across the counter to Carol. "Could you make the chocolate sheet cake and decorate it with a golf or fishing theme and this inscription?"

"I'd be delighted to. Bridget will be in at 11. I'll start it then."

"Perfect. Now I'd better finish our usual stock so I can get to work on the pastries for this order." Laura focused on her recipes and was grateful when Molly appeared and carried the trays to the display case. Laura didn't need to get sucked into any conversations about the football team. As it was, with this new order to fill, she might not finish in time to attend this afternoon's practice, and she'd promised Brody she would watch out for Henry.

While Laura was simultaneously watching the timer for the parlies in the oven and rolling out the dough for shortbread, Trent snuck into the kitchen from the café, a cup of coffee in his hand. "Good morning, sunshine. May I take you to dinner?"

She blew a hank of hair from in front of her face. "I would love that, but I'm afraid it won't work today."

"Football practice?"

"Actually, that'd be over by dinnertime. However, I don't know if I can go to that today either. I have a massive order that has to go out tomorrow morning, and I'll be baking late to fill it."

A slow, crooked smile crept to Trent's lips as he leaned against the doorframe and casually hooked one foot over the other, all the while watching her intently. "That sounds like a job that could use a taste tester."

She laughed aloud at the unexpected comeback.

"And since you have to eat to keep your strength up," he continued, "I propose I bring us takeout. Then I can help you bake, or at least keep you company."

Warmth filled her at his generous offer. "Do you promise not to distract me?"

"As long as I get to sample the goods," he bargained.

"Deal."

"Great. I'll bring the food around six. Should I bring enough for Henry?"

"I'm not sure what his plans are. Can I let you know later?"

"Sure thing. If nothing else, I'll get something you can take home for him that'll reheat well."

The timer for the parlies went off, so Laura pulled them from the oven. She popped a couple of the fragrant, spiced cookies into a paper sack, then offered it to Trent. "To tide you over until supper."

He inhaled appreciatively, then raised an eyebrow. "I'm not sure I can wait that long for more."

She laughed, then wagged a finger at him. "Remember, you promised not to distract me. I can't be putting salt in for sugar."

"I'll be on my best behavior." He straightened and solemnly held up three fingers, but a mirthful twinkle lit his green eyes. "Scout's honor."

At a knock on the shop's back door, Laura poked her head into the hallway and called, "Come on in, Trent. The door's unlocked." Then she hurried back to the counter to finish laminating her pastry dough, the process of layering butter between sheets of dough to achieve optimal flakiness in the finished product.

A moment later, a familiar female voice asked, "Where's Henry?"

The unexpected visitor made Laura jump. "Adina, what are you doing here?" Did her niece miss her family so much that she'd skipped studying and made the long trek from Marquette to visit her brother? Or . . . "Is something wrong at school?"

"Not with my school." The pretty young woman crossed her arms. "What's going on *here*?"

The accusatory tone grated on Laura's nerves. Granted, she was fairly sure Brody was behind Adina's impromptu visit—and Adina probably wasn't too happy about being asked to play spy. "You mean with the football team?"

"That, and with Henry." Adina shrugged her large purse off her shoulder and let it drop to the closest counter. "I went to the school to watch his practice."

Laura tensed. He hadn't responded to her texts earlier about dinner, but she'd written it off as teenage obliviousness, that he'd think about supper when he was hungry for it. "Wasn't he there?"

"Oh, he was. I talked to him afterward, before he headed to the locker room. I told him I would wait for him because I planned to stay over tonight. That's okay, right?"

"Of course you can stay," Laura said. "That's never even a question. I'm afraid I won't be home for a few hours, though. I have a big order to finish. Carol stayed to help as long as she could, but she had another commitment this evening and I told her not to cancel." Laura knew she was babbling, but it seemed better than facing Adina's questions about Henry. "My friend Trent is bringing me dinner here. You're welcome to join us."

Adina barely suppressed a grin at the word "friend." "Speaking of 'friends,' apparently Henry stood me up for some girl named Amy. He said he'd come over here with me once he showered, but he never came out of the locker room. I asked his teammates what happened, and they said he got a text from Amy and left through the locker room's other door after his shower."

He ditched his own sister for Amy? Laura frowned. "I'm sorry to hear that."

Adina shrugged. "No big deal. I think it's cute Henry has a girl. And considering how much he used to tease me about my boyfriends in high school, it makes sense that he didn't tell me he was leaving. Besides, love makes you do dumb things, like stand up your sister."

"You think?" Henry had to know his sister would be annoyed when he didn't meet her. Then again, maybe annoying his sister had been the point. Laura chuckled, recalling plenty of times Brody had done as much to her.

The back door opened. "Dinner's here," Trent announced as he entered the kitchen carrying two oversize paper bags from Lucky Ox, the local Chinese restaurant.

"Smells amazing," Adina said.

He smiled in greeting. "You must be Laura's niece. I can see the resemblance."

"This is Adina," Laura said. "She'll be eating Henry's dinner. She drove up to visit with him, but he's pulled a disappearing act."

Trent set the bags on the counter. "Disappeared? Should we be worried?"

Laura's insides warmed at the concern in his voice. The widower had a college-age son, Jeremy, so he knew a thing or two about the trouble teenage boys could be. "I don't think so. It sounds as if he gave Adina the slip so he could spend time with a girl."

Adina crossed her arms. "That's the thanks I get for driving all the way here to congratulate him on his success."

Laura's eyes widened. "Is that really why you came? Your father didn't put you up to it?"

Adina's cheeks flushed, and she lifted one shoulder in a noncommittal shrug.

"It's okay," Laura assured. "I can't blame him." The whole situation had her worried too, but she wasn't about to admit as much to Adina. Instead, she changed the subject. "I'm ready for a break." She sniffed appreciatively. "Those egg rolls smell amazing. Let's dig in."

After they ate, Adina headed to Laura's house to study while Trent stayed behind at Bread on Arrival to keep Laura company—and sample a pastry or two Laura deemed subpar. By the time Laura arrived home, Adina was sleeping on the sofa and Henry was asleep—or at least pretending to be—in his room.

She supposed she'd have to wait until morning to address his inconsiderate behavior. She sighed. This parenting thing was more exhausting than baking over 300 pastries in a single afternoon.

Wednesday morning, both Adina and Henry were still sleeping when Laura was ready to leave for the bakehouse. Laura left Adina a note inviting her to stop by before she returned to Marquette.

Adina arrived at nine. "I drove Henry to school. He claims Amy is nothing more than a friend, but I don't believe him for a second. His ears turned beet red when he said it."

Laura felt oddly comforted that Henry wasn't only lying to his aunt, though it was troubling that he was lying at all. *Maybe the boy really is just in denial.*

"Anyway, he doesn't sound worried about the things happening to the team," Adina went on, "so I'll let Dad know everything is good."

"I appreciate that." Laura boxed up a selection of Empire biscuits, parlies, Scottish snowballs, and shortbread, then handed it to Adina. "For the road."

Adina gave her a warm hug. "You're the best. It's a good thing I'm not going to Superior Bay College and staying here too."

Laura raised an eyebrow. "Why's that?"

"I'd be big as a house by Thanksgiving." With another hug and a wave goodbye, Adina left.

At a quarter to ten, the kitchen phone rang. Laura ignored it, thinking Molly would pick up the extension in the office. But on the fifth ring, she snatched it up. "Good morn—"

"You gave me the wrong address," Hamish groused before she could finish her greeting.

"Address for what?"

"For the retirement cake and sixty boxes of pastries."

Laura's breath caught in her throat. The deadline for that delivery was fifteen minutes away. She flipped through the carbon copies on the memo book by the phone. She recited the address she'd written. "I got the impression it was a business since it's a retirement party."

"Aye, it's a storefront all right. It's the old record store that went out of business eight years ago." The sound of rattling metal came across the line as Hamish jiggled a security gate. "The place is padlocked and completely deserted. Lass, you've been hoodwinked."

"That can't be!" Laura cried. "I *must* have written down the address wrong." She shook her head, vaguely recalling the fact that she'd double-checked the address with the customer. "Give me a minute. I'll contact the customer and call you right back."

Laura disconnected from Hamish and dialed the woman's contact number. No one picked up. Voice mail didn't kick in.

After eight rings, Laura clanked the receiver back into its cradle and groaned in frustration. "Why isn't she answering?"

"Why isn't who answering?" Molly asked as she entered the kitchen. After Laura explained what was going on, Molly reasoned, "When her cake doesn't show up by ten, I'm sure she'll call us."

Laura relaxed a fraction. "That's true. I'll tell Hamish to finish his other deliveries and we can call him when we have the correct address for this order."

Ten o'clock came and went. At eleven o'clock, Hamish called to say he was finished with the other deliveries. Molly told him to bring the undeliverable boxes back to the bakehouse and they'd store them in the cooler, then decided she'd try the client's number again.

This time someone answered.

"This is Bread on Arrival," Molly explained. "We have your or—"

The person on the other end of the phone cut off her explanation, no doubt with a rant about the cake not being delivered on time. Laura grimaced.

Molly recited the number on the notepad to the person on the other end of the line. At the person's response, Molly blanched. She thanked them and hung up. "Did you take a deposit for this order?" she asked Laura.

Laura pinched her fingers to her temples in a vain attempt to massage away the headache creeping in. "No. I was so distracted, I didn't think to ask."

"The gentleman who answered the phone informed me it was a pay phone on Thistle Street," Molly explained.

Carol stepped into the kitchen with Trent right behind her. "Now we've been pranked?"

"I don't think any of us are amused," Molly said grimly. "We'll have to offer a half-price deal to sell all these before they go stale."

"They'll stay fresh for about a week," Laura said. "That gives us a little time."

Molly nodded. "I'll put the word out on our social media pages."

"With Thanksgiving around the corner, I'm sure they'll be snapped up," Carol said. "Advertise that they freeze well."

"Good idea." Molly pulled out her phone to write up a post.

"Ugh," Laura groaned, unable to keep the misery from her voice. "This is all my fault."

"Nonsense," Carol said. "It could've happened to any of us." She gave Laura a hug. "Don't beat yourself up."

Laura shook her head. "How am I supposed to keep Henry safe if I can't even recognize a prank when it's being played on me?"

Trent cleared his throat. "That pay phone isn't too far from my shop. It's outside the convenience store on Thistle and Loch Ness Lane, which is right next to the high school."

Laura frowned. "So you think it was a high school kid?"

Trent paused. "Back when I had a desk job and traveled frequently, Jeremy once called my secretary and made an appointment to see me because he thought I was too busy to make time for him." He shrugged. "Maybe Henry is doing the opposite."

"What do you mean?" Laura asked.

"You told me last night that he might be embarrassed about your involvement with finding the prankster," Trent continued. "He could have figured this would keep you too preoccupied to investigate. For one day at least."

"It did do that." Laura frowned. "But the caller was definitely female." *Amy?*

Laura closed her eyes and took a deep breath, then slowly released it. She didn't want to believe it possible that Henry had anything to do with this. It wasn't like him at all. Then again, a teenage boy might think it was a lark, not realizing it would cost the bakehouse a lot more than her time if they couldn't sell all the goods.

Molly's phone dinged with an incoming text. She checked the screen and smiled. "I've got good news. Fergus saw my post, and he'll take fifty boxes for an event tonight."

"That's fantastic," Carol said. "I can take the rest out front. Any that we don't sell we can bring to this weekend's tournament for the boys."

"I'd still like to identify our prankster," Laura declared. "This could be connected to the attacks on the team. If the perp figured we were getting too close to outing her, she would want to distract us."

"I'll pay a visit to the convenience store," Trent volunteered. "Most convenience stores have video surveillance. With any luck, they captured an image of your caller."

"You're a lifesaver." Suddenly overcome by appreciation for her friends' cheerful support, Laura took a deep breath and smiled. Everything was going to be okay. With friends like these, how could it not be?

Trent burst through the bakehouse door as Laura, Molly, and Carol were at the front counter discussing closing duties with Bridget.

He waved a piece of paper in the air. "I have a picture of your caller. Only one person used the pay phone Tuesday morning."

Carol bustled around the counter and locked the front door, switching their sign to *Closed*. "Is it someone we know?"

"Hard to tell." Trent laid the image on a bistro table. While Bridget bused tables, the rest of them gathered around to scrutinize it. "I captured this from their video and zoomed in on her. It's pretty grainy, I'm afraid."

Laura frowned at the image, which showed the person from behind. "That Loch Mallaig High hoodie she's wearing makes it impossible to see any distinguishing features. If I hadn't heard her voice, I wouldn't even be able to say it was a woman from the picture."

"True," Trent said. "It was more obvious from the way she moved."

"What did her voice sound like?" Carol asked. "Like any of the girls you've talked to at Henry's practices, maybe?"

Laura tried to replay the voice in her mind. "It was muffled, as if she had a cold. It wasn't familiar."

"She could have been disguising her voice," Molly suggested. "Maybe she held a cloth over the receiver."

"I know you've dismissed him as a suspect, but maybe we need to reassess Brendan," Carol said. "If he's behind the pranks, his sister might have pulled this stunt to get us off his scent."

"Or maybe his sister is the trickster," Trent proposed.

"That had crossed our minds," Laura said. "She's angry enough at the football team for the way they treat her brother, but the itching powder prank and the equipment failure heaped more criticism on him, and the tainted water made him sick. I don't think she'd take that risk with her brother."

Carol nodded agreement. "Jenny knows the Lancashire kids from school. She said Brendan is a little developmentally delayed, so

I imagine his sister has seen him get picked on most of her life. Jenny says he's the sweetest kid you'd ever meet."

"What does Tina drive?" Trent asked. "The person who made the call drove up to the pay phone in a dark-colored, early-2000s Ford Taurus."

"I know someone who drives a hunter-green Taurus." Bridget set down her bus pan with a resounding thud. "Beth Templeton."

16

Laura tugged off her apron. "We need to pay Ms. Templeton a visit." She emitted a disgusted snort. "I had a feeling she wasn't what she seemed. And she had the opportunity to instigate every prank."

"Why would she?" Carol asked.

"My guess is that she did it for Parish," Laura answered.

"She must not have told him," Bridget put in. "It would explain why he drank the poisoned water. He didn't know she'd tampered with it."

"But why would she pull the stunts anonymously?" Molly asked. "I could see her doing it if she was in love with Parish or if he was paying her off, but she seems to be interested in Officer Murdoch. And she certainly wouldn't want to encourage him to investigate if she was behind the pranks."

"I wouldn't put it past her," Laura said. "I think she flirts with him precisely so he won't suspect her."

"If you're going over there to confront her, you'd better call Murdoch and have him meet you," Carol said.

"Us," Molly corrected. "We can't let her go alone."

"Are you sure?" Laura eyed the dirty café.

"Absolutely," Carol and Molly agreed at the same time.

"I'll finish cleanup," Bridget volunteered.

"Hang on a second," Molly said. "I'll run up to the office and print the invoice for the big order." She chuckled. "That will floor her if she did call it in."

While Molly went upstairs, Laura called the police station and asked for Murdoch, but he wasn't in. Wilma Guthrie, the receptionist, took Laura's number and, after failing to pry more details out of Laura, said she'd have him call her back.

"Do you want me to come with you to the school?" Trent offered. "I don't need to be back to my shop for another twenty minutes."

"That's okay," Laura assured. "It'll be three against one as it is. I doubt she'll give us any trouble."

Trent squeezed Laura's arm affectionately. "If you're sure. Please be careful. It sounds as if this woman could have a screw loose."

Bridget laughed. "Could be a side effect of teaching teenagers. In fact, maybe all of this is about getting revenge on problem students. Teens can be nasty." Straightening, she gave a winning smile. "Not that I would know from personal experience."

Carol grinned. "You're a model employee, so I'm sure you have always been a model student."

Molly dashed down the stairs with Angus. "I'm going to drive separately and take Angus to the dog park while we're in the vicinity." She waved a piece of paper. "I've got the invoice. Let's go."

A few minutes later, Molly parked beside Laura and Carol in the high school parking lot. A police cruiser was parked a few spaces away.

"Murdoch must be here already," Laura said as she and Carol met up with Molly.

"There he is." Carol pointed toward a uniformed officer at the edge of the football field.

"And that's Beth with him." Molly held out the invoice to Laura. "Would you like to do the honors?"

"With pleasure." Laura strode across the parking lot and straight up to the pair. "Excuse me, Beth. I believe this is yours." She handed over the invoice.

As Beth glanced at the paper, her confused expression morphed into one more akin with fear and her instant blush gave her away. "I-I don't know what you're talking about. I didn't order any of this."

"Just because the address you gave us made them undeliverable doesn't mean you don't have to pay for them," Laura said sternly. "We prepared them in good faith."

"But I didn't order anything." Beth's high-pitched denial rang false.

"Someone must have pretended to be her," Officer Murdoch said in her defense. "You can't expect her to pay for something she didn't order."

"I know she ordered it. I have photographic proof." Laura withdrew the picture from her pocket.

Beth stiffened, but before she could respond, Murdoch took the photo and studied it. "That could be anybody." A call came over the radio pinned to his shoulder—dispatch calling him about a car accident. "I've got to go."

"You can't yet." Laura snatched back the photo. "We know who—"

"I have to. Thanks for the tip, Beth." Murdoch strode toward his cruiser.

So much for wheedling a confession out of Beth in front of him. "What tip was that, Beth?" Laura asked. "Are your tips like your bakery orders—meant to distract?"

Beth wilted. "I'm sorry. I'll pay for the order." She clawed open her purse and pulled all the cash from her wallet, then held it toward Laura. "Take this as a down payment. I'll get you the rest tomorrow. Just please don't tell Dalziel what I did."

"Are you kidding me?" Laura scoffed. "You were the one who urged him to find the prankster."

"And we think it's time he learns it's you," Carol added.

Beth jerked back. "Me? I didn't prank the football team. Yes, I called in this bogus order, but that's all. I was trying to keep you busy so Dalziel could investigate without you getting in the way." Her gaze skittered toward his cruiser speeding off. Affection lit her eyes. "Haven't you seen how much more confidence he exudes? Like the way he stood up for me after you accused me of placing an undeliverable order?"

"You'll forgive me if I don't believe you." Laura strained to keep her tone even. "I think you realized we were on to you and sent us the order to sideline us while you wheedled your way deeper into Dalziel's trust."

"No," Beth insisted. "That's not it at all."

"Come on," Molly said. "As a teacher, you would have had easy access to the boys' locker room to coat their shoulder pads with itching powder so your good friend Marcus Parish would win the tournament."

"That's ridiculous," Beth shot back. "Marcus is an acquaintance at best. Gym teachers don't exactly have a lot in common with English teachers, unless one of their players fails to make the minimum grade required to play."

Ignoring Beth's objection, Molly continued, "So you learned Parish's team would play in the district finals. Given your gift for sweet-talking men, I'm sure you would have had no problem accessing the storage room to sabotage the practice equipment."

Beth crossed her arms. "I don't have to listen to this. You have no proof of any of it."

"We have proof you placed the phony order," Carol said. "When we show it to Murdoch, whom do you think he'll believe about the rest?"

Beth held up both hands. "I didn't do all of that! I would never."

"It would have been easy enough for you to slip under the bus before it left the school and nick the gas line." Laura wiped her finger over a smudge on Beth's jacket. "Is that a grease stain?"

Beth snapped her arm back indignantly. "It most certainly is not."

"When that delay tactic didn't work and our team still made it to the final game against Parish, I'm sure it would have been easy for you to taint our team's water," Laura mused.

Beth shook her head vigorously. "This is ridiculous. I am an *English* teacher. I wouldn't know a gas line from a jumper cable." Her eyes suddenly widened. She straightened. "I couldn't have cut the gas line. I had a dentist appointment that afternoon."

Molly rolled her eyes. "You're forgetting we talked to you before the game, *before* our team's bus arrived."

"That's because I drove straight there from my appointment." Beth dug through her purse once more, then victoriously withdrew a folded piece of paper. "This is the receipt for my appointment. It shows the time." She unfolded it and held it out for them. "I left Loch Mallaig at one o'clock, before the team's bus arrived at the school to pick them up." She pointed to the time stamp on the credit card receipt stapled to the invoice. "And it was almost three o'clock when I paid for the cleaning and left. By then, the bus would have been long gone."

"You could have happened by the same rest stop en route," Carol countered.

"I was driving from a town twenty minutes farther away," Beth said. "The only way I would have caught up to them was if they'd already broken down. As it was, I didn't pass them, so I must have taken a different road." She produced another receipt, this one for gas, dated the same afternoon. "Here's the address of the gas station I used."

"Okay," Laura conceded. "So, you didn't cut their gas line."

Beth adopted a pleading expression. "I didn't do that or any of the other things. I was trying to help Dalziel succeed because I really like him. I heard through the grapevine that he's never had a girlfriend, and I think it's because he's insecure. I just want to give him some self-confidence so he'll ask me out. Please don't tell him what I did to you."

The Bakehouse Three stepped aside to consider her argument.

"I believe her," Carol whispered. "She's clearly head over heels for Murdoch, but that's no motive for pulling these pranks."

"It's also no excuse for manipulating his investigation," Molly said.

Carol grimaced. "It would really embarrass him if he found out what she did."

Laura heaved a sigh. "I suppose if she pays us for her bogus order, at least the part we didn't sell to Fergus, I'm willing to forgo telling Murdoch. But it's for his sake, not hers."

"So we're agreed?" Molly asked.

Laura held up a finger. "With one stipulation. I don't want to see her at any more of our team's football practices or games. I don't care what excuse she needs to give Murdoch to explain her absence."

The women delivered their edict to Beth, who accepted their terms with relief. "I promise I'll stay away from the team," she said. "And I'll be at your shop first thing tomorrow morning with the rest of your money."

"You'd better," Carol said sternly, "or the deal is off."

Laura had to stifle a grin at Carol's blustery show, considering she'd been the first to soften under Beth's plea.

Beth hurried away and the women shifted their attention to the football practice.

"The stands are filled with more parents today than earlier this week," Laura observed.

"I don't think those are all parents," Molly said. "I don't recognize half of them from any other games."

"They could be spies from teams the Loons will face in their next tournament," Carol speculated.

Laura pulled out her cell phone and began snapping pictures of the spectators. "We can compare these to the ones taken by the yearbook photographer. Hopefully we'll find some clue to our prankster's identity." She shook her head solemnly. "Because right now it feels like we're back to square one."

Before leaving the school, Laura had sent Henry a text telling him she was making spaghetti for dinner—his favorite—and inviting him to bring Amy along. She'd never expected him to actually do it, so she was surprised but truly pleased when he arrived home just before six with Amy in tow.

"This is my friend, Amy," he said by way of introduction.

The girl nervously tucked a wayward strand of her brunette hair behind her ear and scarcely made eye contact with her equally dark brown eyes. "Thank you for having me, Ms. Donovan."

"Call me Laura. And the pleasure is mine."

The kids set the table while Laura grated cheese over the garlic bread she'd made. Whether it was nerves or inattention, Henry seemed to drop more utensils and napkins than made it to the table.

"Butterfingers like that could cost you the game," Laura quipped.

Henry turned redder than the spaghetti sauce, and Laura immediately regretted teasing him. She supposed she should be grateful Amy didn't make him that nervous when he was on the field. Then again, maybe it was Laura herself who was making him nervous. Was he worried about what she would think of his girlfriend? Was that why he'd taken so long to introduce them?

They ate a few bites in silence before Laura concluded it would be up to her to initiate a conversation. "So Amy, what is your favorite subject in school?"

"Chemistry," she enthused without hesitation.

"That's great," Laura said with a fleeting glance at Henry. "An interest in science will serve you well when it comes to finding a career."

Henry glowered at Laura, no doubt guessing that she was thinking about the scientific knowledge needed to make itching powder and to poison the water canteen.

"Definitely," Amy went on, clearly warming to the subject. "I love science and math—always have. I want to go to the University of Michigan for biochemistry. I'd love to work on research that helps protect the fish and plant life in the Great Lakes."

"Wow, that's wonderful," Laura said, genuinely impressed. "I love that you have clear goals for your studies."

Henry seemed to relax a little. "Yeah, it's awesome."

Amy smiled at him with unabashed adoration. "Most of our classmates think I'm nuts. All they want to do is get decent enough grades to get into college so they can party."

Laura nodded. "I was like you. Everyone called me a bookworm or an egghead."

"Yeah, I always got 'teacher's pet' a lot when I was younger," Amy said. "Now it's words I shouldn't repeat."

"Is that what happened outside the movie theater the other night?" Laura asked.

"Sort of," Amy said. "A kid I used to tutor called me something nasty when he saw us. I stopped tutoring him after he was caught cheating with the study notes I helped him make."

"Good for you," Laura said. "Better he learns cheating doesn't pay when he's young."

"That kid's trouble," Henry said. "He's always up to no good."

"Nice guys do stuff like that sometimes too." Laura tried to make the remark sound offhanded. "I've noticed a few of the football players pick on Brendan, call him names."

"Oh yeah," Amy agreed. "They can be awful. I know from experience."

Henry flashed Laura another glower, but she ignored him and said, "The team's mascot, Kit, seemed to think the itching powder prank would teach them to show Brendan a little more respect."

"Brendan didn't put itching powder on our uniforms," Henry countered. "He's too nice a guy."

"I wouldn't have blamed him if he had, though," Amy said, her expression darkening. "There have been days when I would've done anything to stop being bullied."

Anything? Laura's heart hiccupped at Amy's tone. *Like maybe pretend to date a football player so you could get revenge on the rest of the team?*

The next night, Laura went out to the field to wish Henry well in the first game of the regionals tournament.

"Did you see who we're playing?" he exclaimed, his eyes gleaming. "My old school! I know all their plays and strategies."

"Don't get cocky," she warned. "I'm sure they've changed a few things this season."

"Maybe," Henry said, "but Coach Bassett showed us a video of their last game and their plays were the same as always."

"But remember, the other team will have been doing their homework too. We saw a lot of unfamiliar faces at your practice yesterday. I wouldn't be surprised if they were spies for the teams you could face in the tournament." Laura had spent some time studying photos from the practice and the last tournament, but she hadn't seen any overlap aside from parents of team members.

Henry grinned. "Stop worrying, Aunt Laura. I'll be fine. And Coach has come up with some cool tweaks to our own plays to keep the other team guessing."

"Good." She gave him a quick hug. "Have fun."

"I will." He pulled away and dashed back to his team.

Molly handed Laura a hot cocoa when she rejoined their group in the stands. "I don't know how the boys will be able to hold on to the ball in these temperatures," Molly said.

Laura shivered as the sun slid below the horizon and the air temperature seemed to instantly drop another few degrees.

"I've seen them play in worse," Fergus put in. "Snow isn't unheard of."

"Officer Murdoch is here." Laura pointed to the casually dressed officer three rows down and two sections over. "No sign of Beth."

"I think she'll keep her promise to stay away," Carol said.

"Of course," Molly said, drawing out the words, "if nothing more happens to the team tonight, that won't look good for her either."

"My gut's telling me Coach Bassett was right, and it was all Parish's doing," Carol said. "Now that his team is out of the running, I think we've seen the end of that unpleasantness."

"I hope you're right," Laura said.

The game soon began and within minutes, Henry scored Loch Mallaig's first touchdown. The fans surged to their feet and roared their approval. Henry saluted his opponents as he ran back to the bench.

"His old teammates don't seem impressed," Molly said wryly.

Laura laughed. "They probably thought the game would be a walk in the park when they heard one of their former second-string players was our star running back."

After Loch Mallaig successfully scored their extra point, Henry's former coach called a time-out and approached the nearest referee.

Laura took out the small pair of binoculars she'd brought and focused on the men. "No way. My lipreading isn't great, but I think he's accusing us of bringing Henry in as a ringer."

The pair approached Coach Bassett, and a moment later he laughed heartily.

"I suspect he plans on reminding the other coach that Henry was a second-string player on his team," Fergus said.

Laura adjusted the focus on her binoculars. "The three of them are walking over to someone else now."

"The person who makes the final call, maybe?" Carol speculated.

"The authorities already declared Henry's school transfer acceptable before the last tournament," Laura said, "so they shouldn't be allowed to reverse their decision now."

A moment later, the game announcer reported that play would resume with Loch Mallaig kicking to their opponents. Laura divided her time between watching the game and using her binoculars to keep an eye on the area around Loch Mallaig's bench. There was no canteen of water, she'd noticed. Instead, the players had been supplied with several cases of bottled water. Brendan dutifully handed them out, leaving the job of cracking the seal to each player. And in deference to parental concerns, Bread on Arrival's offer to bring food for the team was rejected in favor of packaged snacks.

By halftime, Loch Mallaig was ahead by three touchdowns and Larry the Loon had the crowd on their feet and cheering with wild abandon. While the others watched the halftime show, Laura kept her binoculars focused on the team bench. Several players went to the locker room, but the coach had already declared they'd have a guard posted and no one else would be permitted inside.

"Relax," Carol said close to Laura's ear, so she could be heard over the sound of the marching band. "The coach is taking their safety seriously. And I can't imagine what anyone could do to them now to turn this game around for Henry's old school."

Laura muffled a sigh. *I can imagine a few things.* Still, she tried not to think about the possible scenarios that had played through her mind and kept her awake half the night.

The third quarter began with an upset, with their opponents scoring a touchdown on the kickoff ball.

"Wow," Molly said, "their coach must have given them some pep talk at halftime."

The roar of the fans on the other side of the field was more deafening than Loch Mallaig's had been for their goals. Signs burst into the air, encouraging their team to greater feats. Not to be outdone, Larry the Loon circled his wings to stir their fans into a rallying cry.

Henry caught the kick and charged past three players and across yard line after yard line before finally being tackled. Laura cringed at the impact, but Henry popped back to his feet in no time.

By the end of the game, Loch Mallaig had scored two more field goals and trounced their opponents by twenty points.

"He's going to the state semifinals!" Laura shouted into her phone to her brother's voice mail, trying to be heard above the noise of the roaring crowd.

Later, as Laura and Henry walked to her car, they passed a few players from his old school.

"Hey guys, how's it going?" Henry said. "Mr. Wise still teaching science?" He made a funny face.

"We don't talk to people who forget where their loyalties should be, Donovan," snarled the largest boy in the group.

"It's not as if I had a choice about switching schools," Henry countered. "My parents are out of the country and my aunt lives in Loch Mallaig."

"You sold us out," another player accused. "Told your coach all our plays."

Henry's cheeks colored.

"You'd better watch your back, Donovan." A third player glared at Henry and slammed his closed fist into the palm of his other hand in a threatening gesture. "Nobody likes a traitor."

Laura's stomach filled with ice as she watched the opponents veer off and disappear into the night. Did Henry have a new threat to worry about?

"I've been looking forward to putting my feet up and finishing my book," Laura said to Henry after they'd finished their lunch Sunday afternoon.

"No way," he replied. "You have to come to the school, Aunt Laura. The whole town will be there."

She hid a smile. "I thought you preferred I stay out of things."

Henry rolled his eyes. "This is a celebration. It's been thirty years since the town made the state semifinals."

"Isn't this a party for the young people?" Laura wasn't sure why she was being contrary about going. She had resigned herself to staying home, thinking Henry wouldn't want his aunt around cramping his style. His eagerness for her to attend surprised her.

"No, it's for everyone. They want to publicly recognize the players and coaches and stuff."

"Well, if you're sure you want me there, I suppose I could come. I can send your parents videos and photos."

Henry hugged her. "You'll have fun. You'll see."

"Can I ask Trent to join us?"

"You don't need my permission to bring a date, Aunt Laura, but for the record, I'm cool with it."

"Good to know."

Half an hour later, Henry, Trent, and Laura wove through the crowd gathered around a makeshift stage in the center of the high school's football field until they reached Molly and Fergus.

"I didn't expect to see you two here," Laura said.

"Fergus insisted we *had* to be here." Molly playfully slugged Henry's shoulder. "Your nephew is part of Loch Mallaig history in the making now."

Carol bustled over to them with Harvey at her side. "Here you are.

I thought I'd never find you in this crowd. What a great turnout!"

"Thanks for coming," Henry said.

"Our pleasure, young man," Harvey said. "Thanks for inviting us."

Laura did a double take. "You invited them?"

"Of course," Henry answered as though his actions were obvious.

"What's going on?" Molly whispered to Laura as Henry hurried off to join Amy and his teammates at the foot of the stage.

"Wait and see." The twitch of Fergus's beard said he knew the answer to her question.

Carol nudged Laura's arm and nodded toward the fringes of the crowd, where Beth Templeton stood. "Does this count as being at one of the school's football events?"

Reflexively, Laura tensed. "As one of the school's teachers, I'm sure she felt obligated to attend."

Trent must have sensed Laura's apprehension, because he leaned over and whispered, "Relax. It's okay."

Laura shook her shoulders and took a deep breath. It wasn't as if she still believed Beth was behind the attacks on the team, but still not knowing who was to blame was keeping her on edge.

"They're starting," Molly announced.

Mayor Tavish Calhoun climbed the stairs to the stage and unhooked the microphone from the stand at the podium. "Good afternoon, Loch Mallaig!" he boomed. The stout retired dentist, his red hair aflame in the autumn sunshine, beamed at the crowd. "We're here to celebrate the success of our very own Loch Mallaig Loons."

The crowd broke into applause, whoops, and whistles—except Coach Nelson, who stood in front of Laura and her friends. "My team could make it to State too if the school invested as much in our equipment as it's spent on the football team," the track coach grumbled to the high school principal beside him.

"Now's not the time to discuss your funding grievances," Mr. Groves replied.

"If not now, there will be nothing left," Nelson argued. "You've already reneged on your promise to distribute the poinsettia fundraiser money according to the portion of orders brought in by each team."

"You yourself said it wouldn't be fair."

"That was before my team worked their tails off to bring in the lion's share of orders while the football team did nothing."

"They were rather preoccupied practicing for regionals."

Mr. Nelson snorted derisively, and the principal excused himself and made his way to the stage.

"Can you believe the way Karl is gloating?" Nelson complained to the woman on his other side.

Laura cocked her head and assessed the football coach. Bassett didn't appear to be gloating to her, merely elated with his team's success.

Mayor Calhoun invited Principal Groves up to present the team. The principal gave a short speech commending the coaches and players on their hard work and courage in the face of unusual adversity.

"That's code for 'sabotage,'" Harvey murmured to Carol and Laura. "It's the kind of political doublespeak reporters have to contend with interpreting every day. Makes me glad I'm retired."

Carol hugged her husband's arm. "Ah, admit it. You had fun researching Marcus Parish for Laura. You had that gleam in your eye you used to get when you were on the trail of something big."

Laura frowned. "Only it didn't pan out that way."

"I'd also like to personally thank Bread on Arrival," the principal went on, "for their contribution to the team in providing snacks for games and for tonight's celebration."

Laura knit her brow and swung her gaze from Carol to Molly, but they both appeared equally confused.

"I don't know what he's talking about," Molly said.

Fergus's face split into a wide grin. "I do. I donated the pastries I bought this week."

Molly's eyes narrowed suspiciously. "Is that what you intended to do with them all along?"

He gave a sheepish shrug.

"And what would you have done if the team didn't win the tournament?" Molly sounded equal parts admiring and stunned.

"Given them as welcome gifts to visitors staying at the lodge, I suppose," Fergus answered. "I felt confident betting on our boys to bring home a win, though."

Chuckling, Laura thanked him. "I guess Henry knew about this, and that's why it was so important to him we all be here."

"He's very proud to be the nephew of Bread on Arrival's chief baker," Fergus confirmed, and Laura's heart warmed at the affirmation.

Next, Coach Bassett invited his team to join him on the stage as he announced their names and positions. The cheerleading squad, accompanied by Kit in his mascot costume, stood in front of the stage facing the crowd, leading cheers for each player. For several of the players, Bassett noted important plays they'd made in the deciding game.

Seemingly propelled forward by the players around him, Brendan arrived at the stage steps behind Henry, but Bassett motioned him to step aside.

An angry female voice behind Laura hissed, "How can he treat Brendan like that?"

Laura glanced back and wasn't surprised to see Brendan's sister.

"Brendan works every bit as hard as the players," Tina ranted to her friend as Brendan joined her. "He never misses a practice. He gets there before them to set up and stays late to ensure everything is put away."

Brendan shrugged. "It's no big deal."

"And a football game wouldn't be the same without our amazing cheerleaders," Bassett went on, motioning for the squad to join the players on stage.

Instead of following the cheerleaders, Kit made a beeline toward Brendan and dragged him along toward the stage. Once there, Kit got the principal's attention and whispered something to him.

A moment later, Principal Groves reclaimed the mic and invited the crowd to cheer for Coach Bassett and his assistant coaches. He then added, "And last but certainly not least, I'd like to recognize the dedication and hard work of our equipment manager, Brendan Lancashire."

Behind Laura, Tina let out an ear-piercing whistle and clapped wildly. Brendan trudged up the stairs to the stage, as if his feet were coated in heavy cement.

"You've got to give that loon character credit," Harvey observed. "He took initiative."

"And more importantly, he cares about other people's feelings," Carol said.

"Too bad Brendan is so embarrassed by the attention." Laura felt a wave of sympathy for the blushing boy. The poor kid just couldn't seem to catch a break.

A tingle shot down her spine. What if he intended to create his own break? How far would he go to make it happen?

18

"Someone's knocking at the back door," Laura called to her partners from the bakehouse kitchen the next morning.

Molly hurried down the hall. "It's Officer Murdoch," she announced on her way to let him in.

Laura grabbed a tea towel to wipe the flour from her hands as Molly let Officer Murdoch in. At the grim expression on his face, her heart pounded. "Is Henry okay? Please tell me nothing happened to him."

He leveled a stern gaze at Laura. "I need to know where you were between eight and nine o'clock last night."

Laura scrunched her brow in confusion. "Home. Why?"

"What about Henry?" he asked.

"He was home too. What's going on?"

Murdoch's eyes narrowed. "You're sure he didn't borrow your car and go out?"

"Of course I'm sure. What's this all about?"

Carol and Molly flanked Laura, their arms crossed over their chests. "Do you suspect Laura of something?" Carol asked.

"I didn't do anything," Laura declared.

Murdoch sighed, his shoulders relaxing. "I didn't think so. Someone let the air out of Coach Bassett's tires last night, and a neighbor saw a Volkswagen Beetle on the street between those hours."

"And you thought of me?" Laura planted her hands on her hips. "There are other Beetles in Loch Mallaig. Why on earth would you think Henry or I would want to do that to the coach's car?"

"I didn't," Murdoch answered. "Not really. But Henry is on the team, you've been heavily involved with them, and you drive a Beetle. I had to follow this thread. To be honest, if the culprit really wanted to be malicious, he would've taken a knife to the rubber rather than just letting the air out."

"Do you even know if the tires were deflated between eight and nine?" Molly asked.

"No," the officer admitted. "It was some time after seven last night and before six this morning."

Carol shook her head with a cluck of disgust. "That's a pretty big window of opportunity for you to come charging over here to cast aspersions on Laura, simply because she drives a Beetle that might've been in the neighborhood during one hour of that time."

"I'm eliminating suspects, not making accusations," Murdoch countered.

"You weren't exactly friendly about it," Molly chided.

He ducked his head. "I apologize. You three have been helpful with my investigation into the incidents befalling the football team. Unfortunately, it doesn't appear as if our mischief-maker is calling it quits as we'd hoped."

"Oh, he went way past mischief when he graduated from coating uniforms with itching powder to sabotaging practice equipment that could cause serious injury," Laura said.

"Not to mention what poisoning the water canteen could've done," Carol interjected.

"If I were you," Molly said, "I'd be talking to the track-and-field coach. What's his name, Laura?"

"Giles Nelson."

"That's right." Molly returned her attention to Officer Murdoch. "Or maybe it's one of the kids on his team. If you ask me, he sounded more than a little annoyed with Bassett at yesterday's celebration."

"Brendan's sister, Tina, wasn't too pleased with the way Bassett shooed Brendan away from the stage rather than recognizing his contributions along with the team," Carol added.

Murdoch's brow furrowed. "Brendan was recognized."

"Only because Kit dragged him up and spoke to the principal," Laura said. "Bassett didn't acknowledge him. Principal Groves did."

Murdoch jotted the information into his notebook.

"You think the tires were deflated by whoever has been causing trouble for the football team?" Laura clarified.

"It seems likely," he said.

Bridget came in the back door behind Murdoch. "I saw the cruiser outside. What's going on?" When they filled her in on the vandalism to the coach's car, she said, "It rained last night. Did the perp leave behind any shoe prints?"

"He did." Murdoch pulled his cell phone from his pocket and showed her a picture he'd snapped of one. "We estimate it to be a men's size 11, so it probably doesn't belong to Brendan's sister."

Bridget took the phone and zoomed in on the image. "I recognize this tread from my forensics class, when we learned how to make molds of shoe prints. It's from a Converse sneaker. Do you see how defined the prints edges are? The shoes probably aren't that worn."

"Ghillie Me Softly had a sale on those a couple of weeks ago," Laura said. "I remember overhearing Henry asking Brody if he could buy a pair."

"Did he?" Murdoch asked, his voice stern again.

"No, he didn't," Laura answered quickly. "And he didn't take out my car," she repeated for good measure.

"Just checking."

"Patty Ifill, the shoe store manager, is a regular customer," Carol said. "We can ask her if she remembers who bought shoes of that brand in that size, or if she can figure it out from her records."

At the sound of Hamish's old Studebaker Speedster, Nessie, rumbling into the parking lot, Murdoch flipped his notebook closed. "That's okay. I'll pay the shoe store a visit when they open. Thanks for your help, ladies. Have a good day."

As the back door closed behind Murdoch, Laura sighed. "Fat chance of having a good day now that he's raised the specter of our saboteur still on the prowl," she grumbled as the three got back to work.

Three hours later, Molly peeked around the kitchen doorjamb. "Patty from Ghillie Me Softly is here. I'm going to ask her if Murdoch talked to her."

"Be right there." Laura took fresh tartlets out of the oven and set them in a cooling rack, then hurried out to the front counter.

"No, I haven't seen any police officer," Patty, a sturdy brunette, was saying to Molly, "but we aren't open on Mondays, so I haven't been in the shop."

"Do you recall how many of the sneakers you sold when they were on sale a few weeks ago?" Laura asked.

"Oh, quite a few," Patty answered.

"Did you sell any size 11s?" Molly specified.

"I'm sure we did, but I can't recall to whom." Patty took a sip of the coffee Molly had poured her.

"The track coach, Giles Nelson, maybe?" Laura prompted.

Patty shook her head. "No, I would've remembered him. That particular shoe style is most popular with teenagers."

Carol gave a man his change, then joined the conversation. "You live next door to the Lancashires, don't you?"

"That's right," Patty said.

"Do you recall if Brendan bought a pair?" Carol asked.

"I know for certain he didn't. He only wears one brand, and it's not the ones that were on sale. His mom can't get him to try anything else." The woman tapped her chin thoughtfully. "I do remember the football team's quarterback buying a pair. They might have been a size 11. Why do you ask?"

Laura glanced toward the shop's tables, where a few customers were enjoying their purchases, and lowered her voice. "The coach's car tires were deflated, and shoe prints made by that size and brand were found nearby."

"I see," Patty said thoughtfully.

"And I remember your shop recently had a sale on them," Laura added. "I told Officer Murdoch. That's why I imagine he'll talk to you."

"Oh dear. Who would do such a thing? Karl has been so good with the boys. I can't imagine the quarterback, of all people, doing it." Patty's eyes widened. "Ah, that's why you asked about Giles. You think he might." She nodded. "I heard him at the celebration yesterday. His attitude toward Karl is caustic to say the least. If he wears those shoes, he didn't buy them from me. At least not recently. You'll have to check out people's footwear as they come in." She grinned as her gaze roamed over the display case. "I was just going to have coffee, but I've been here long enough to be tempted by these goodies. I'll take a dozen assorted biscuits, please."

"Coming right up." Carol assembled a box to put them in.

As soon as the shoe store manager left with her purchase, Laura said to Carol and Molly, "I think she's right about the QB. I can't think of any motive he'd have to vandalize the coach's car. I could more easily see it from someone like Ben Merrells, the player that the coach demoted to second string, or Frank Aldridge, the guy he cut from the team."

"We know Frank couldn't have poisoned the water, and it's unlikely Merrell would have done it either, let alone sabotaged the bus," Carol countered. "Second string or not, he'd still want to play with his team as far as they could go. Don't you think?"

"That's assuming the attack on the coach's car is connected to the other incidents," Molly added. "It might not be."

"To be honest, that would make me feel a whole lot less worried about Henry," Laura admitted. "I could see Tina deflating the tires. She was furious with the way the coach sidelined her brother yesterday, but unless she wore someone else's shoes to deliberately confuse the police investigation, I doubt it was her."

"Anything's possible, I suppose," Molly said. "I hope Murdoch will speak to both Giles and Tina, given their reaction to Bassett yesterday."

"At least we can do what Patty suggested and scrutinize the shoes people are wearing," Carol said.

"It's worth a shot," Laura said, but deep down, she doubted it would get them any closer to unmasking their menace.

"See?" Laura said to Bridget as they drove into the high school parking lot that afternoon. "I didn't need to let you drag me to Henry's practice. Officer Murdoch is here keeping an eye on things."

"Processing clues is good forensics practice for me," Bridget said breezily. "My professor is impressed that I'm putting the skills he teaches in class to use on a real case. Besides, I told Henry we could do his tutoring session right after practice."

"But what is there to process? Murdoch took the shoe-print picture. All we're doing is searching for someone wearing that kind of shoes."

"Actually, before I started my shift, I zipped over to Coach Bassett's house and made a plaster mold of the imprint."

Laura raised an eyebrow. "You trespassed on a crime scene?"

Bridget rolled her eyes. "It's not as if someone were murdered. They didn't have it cordoned off or anything. In fact, the coach's car was already gone. I recognized a lawn ornament near the shoe print that I'd noticed in Murdoch's photo."

"What do you intend to do if we find someone wearing Converse sneakers? Try to fit their shoe into the mold like Cinderella?"

Bridget grinned. "If need be."

A dramatic sight met them around the side of the bleachers. The quarterback, Jason, held a quivering Moira by the shoulders. She was vigorously shaking her head and trying to pull free. She finally slammed her pompoms into his chest, forcing him to let go. Clearly fighting tears, she stormed back to her cheerleading squad.

"That looked intense," Laura said to Henry, who met her and Bridget by the fence.

Henry nodded. "Jason broke up with Moira last night. That was his lame attempt at an apology. She was at his house when a college scout called, inviting him to play for Michigan State. She said she'd apply to go there too so they could be together. Then his dad told him she was too much of a distraction, and that he needs to focus on his playing. And he got to thinking that she shouldn't pick her college and decide her whole future based on a high school relationship that might not last."

"Ouch," Bridget said. "Not cool to do it right before the fall formal."

"I'm sure she'll have no shortage of new admirers who will be eager to accompany her," Laura said. "In fact, if I'm not mistaken, I think one is already working up the courage." She covertly indicated a blushing Brendan approaching Moira in fits and starts—two steps forward and one step back—his lips moving the entire time as if rehearsing how he'd ask.

"Ooh, that's so cute," Bridget cooed.

Henry was called across the field by the assistant coach, so Bridget and Laura watched Brendan. When he finally faced Moira, he didn't seem to know what to do with his hands. First he moved them about as if he were talking with them, then he stuffed them in his pockets, all the time seemingly talking nonstop to the cheerleader.

Moira's expression changed from one of curiosity to amusement. And when Brendan finally stopped talking long enough to draw a breath, she laughed aloud. "Did Jason put you up to this?" she asked, her voice carrying so that everyone could hear.

Brendan appeared stricken. "N-no, I-I've always liked you," he stuttered, an impediment Laura hadn't observed in him before now.

"Well, sh-sh-she can't go with you," one of the other cheerleaders announced mockingly.

Brendan frowned. "Th-that's for her to decide, Izzy."

"It's impossible," Moira agreed. "Cheerleaders need to be seen on the arms of our players, not their water boy. You're beneath me."

Laura gaped. She knew Moira's parents from church, and she was sure the girl had been brought up better than to treat a boy like that.

Bridget shook her head. "You'd think after the way the QB dumped her, she'd have a little more empathy for Brendan. He may not be her usual type, but that was just cruel."

Brendan retreated and, a moment later, disappeared into the school.

Kit stomped over to Moira. "That was *not* cool."

"Not that you're the expert in that department," Izzy said.

"I know how to show common decency. You should try it sometime," Kit spat back, then headed into the school after Brendan.

"I like that boy's style," Laura said to Bridget.

"Yeah, not too many teenage boys have enough confidence to stand up against the 'cool' kids." Bridget made air quotes to stress that *cool* wouldn't be the descriptor she'd use.

"We'd better get cracking on what we came to do," Laura said. "Practice is already half over."

"Did you notice that there are no kids hanging around to watch the practice like in past weeks?" Bridget scanned the feet of parents sitting in the bleachers. "And none of the parents are wearing incriminating sneakers."

"Maybe Officer Murdoch surveying the area from beside Coach Bassett has something to do with the lack of kids," Laura said.

"Probably. I don't think we're going to catch our sneaker wearer today. At least not here," Bridget said. "We probably have time to walk around to the front of the school to check out the feet of the kids waiting for school buses or hanging out in the parking lot. What do you say?"

"Sure."

But by the time they rounded the building, the last school bus was pulling away from the curb.

"So much for that idea," Laura said, then added wryly, "Maybe we should ask Beth if she knows what size shoes Marcus Parish wears."

"Her promise to you guys to stay away from football practices has got to be killing her," Bridget said as they circled the building back to the field. "Especially today, with Officer Murdoch standing out there."

"I hope he doesn't think she's giving him the cold shoulder," Laura said. "He might give up on the idea of a relationship before it has a chance to bloom."

As they rounded the building, someone standing at one of the classroom windows jerked back into the shadows.

"Was that Beth?" Bridget asked.

Laura squinted at the window, then followed the line of sight the person would have had—a perfect view of Murdoch on the field. "Oh dear. She's got it bad. Do you think I should give her permission to go out and talk to him?"

Bridget chuckled. "Your call."

"As Kit would say, we should show a little common decency." Laura walked to the window and got on her tiptoes to peer inside.

The classroom was dark, with no sign that anyone had been there. "I guess we scared her off."

A chilly breeze stirred, and Laura shivered as she and Bridget continued on. Glancing back at the window then at the football field full of players, she second-guessed herself. Had that really been a lovestruck Beth watching Officer Murdoch—or was the saboteur waiting in the shadows, plotting his or her next sinister move?

19

The week continued much the same way as Monday had transpired, with no new clues, no sign of their sneaker-clad ne'er-do-well, and fortunately, no more pranks. At dinner on Wednesday evening, Henry mentioned hoping Brendan would be back at school in time for their game that weekend.

"He's been absent?" Laura asked, startled.

"No practice or classes," Henry said. "Word is that he's sick."

"Oh dear. I wonder what he has."

"A bruised ego," Henry replied. "He asked the head cheerleader to the fall formal and got the royal brush-off."

"Yes, I saw it happen," Laura admitted. "Poor guy. He couldn't have chosen a more public place to get rejected if he'd tried."

"If only he'd asked a friend for advice first." Henry shook his head. "I would have told him not to bother in the first place, but if he insisted, I would have told him to ask her somewhere more private. Any guy would have."

"Are you his friend?" Laura asked.

Henry gave a noncommittal shrug.

"He doesn't seem to have any, except maybe Kit." She tilted her head. "Maybe you should reach out to him. If he's not at school tomorrow, you could pay him a visit. I can give you a box of cookies from the bakehouse."

Henry grimaced, but didn't say anything.

Laura sympathized with her nephew, who was caught between

compassion and peer pressure. Still, there was a right thing to do here. "I'd hate for him to miss the tournament because of some insensitive girl, wouldn't you?"

Henry sighed. "All right. I'll talk to him."

"Great," Laura said. "You're doing the right thing, Henry."

He gave her a small smile.

Brendan wasn't at school the following day, so between the bakehouse closing and the start of football practice, Laura drove Henry to the Lancashires' home, a neat ranch in a quiet neighborhood.

Laura spied Kit coming out the door as she turned into the driveway. "It seems Kit had the same idea."

Kit was all smiles, making the dimple in his chin more pronounced than ever. He sauntered toward them and Laura lowered her side window. "Brendan will be back on the job for the start of tomorrow's tournament," he announced.

"Great to hear," Laura said. "How'd you convince him?"

"I let him know that I refreshed Moira's memory about what it feels like to be bullied," Kit replied, and Laura realized he must have reminded the cheerleader of Frank's verbal abuse. "She won't be bothering Brendan anymore."

"That's good," Henry said to Laura from the passenger seat.

"It is," Laura murmured, still thinking about Frank.

"I'll see you at practice, Donovan," Kit said, heading down the drive.

"Hey, Kit," Laura called after him. "Do you think Frank would've deflated Coach Bassett's car tires?"

He whirled around, eyes wide as if he were surprised by the theory, but then he nodded thoughtfully. "It's possible."

Laura leaned her head back against the seat and peered through the windshield at the Lancashires' house. "Frank had motive," she muttered, more to herself than Henry. "Losing his place on the team cost him his girl and likely his status with the popular crowd. Yet we know he couldn't have poisoned the water canteen at the district tournament. He was nowhere near the town."

"Who said the same person did everything?" Henry asked. "Did you notice Kit was wearing Converse sneakers?"

She twisted in her seat and craned her neck, but Kit was already out of sight. "Are you sure?"

"Yeah. I'm surprised you didn't notice."

"Me too," Laura admitted. It made perfect sense that Kit might retaliate against Bassett after the way the coach had treated Brendan at Sunday's celebration. Kit was always rising to Brendan's defense. Why wouldn't he take it a step further and actually avenge his friend? And if that was the case, Laura almost hated to call him out on it. After all, the coach always treated Brendan abysmally. Between that and Moira's public rejection, it was no wonder the boy didn't want to go to school.

Laura shook off her reverie. "You were going to talk to Brendan, right?"

Henry rolled his eyes. "Not much point now, is there?"

"It would show some solidarity. You know, in case Brendan's courage wavers when it's time to leave for school in the morning."

"You're right. Back in a minute." Henry climbed out of the car and strode to the front door.

While Henry was inside, Laura's thoughts wandered to Kit and the strong possibility that he was the one who'd deflated Coach Bassett's tires. She smiled. If it was true, then at least she didn't have to worry that their saboteur had started up again.

---✦---

"Laura." Carol poked her head through the bakehouse kitchen door on Friday morning. "Grizela is out front. She says she needs to talk to you."

Laura wiped her hands on her apron and hurried after Carol. "Did she say why?"

"Something about a book."

Grizela wasted no time with pleasantries. She started talking as soon as she saw Laura, gesticulating wildly. "Laura, I don't know why I didn't think to check for the physical books when you asked after them. They showed up in the computer system so I assumed they were on their shelves, you know? Then this morning, an aspiring writer came in wanting one and I couldn't find it on the shelf. But it wasn't signed out either."

Laura had never seen the stern, iron-spined woman so flustered.

"I've spent the last hour combing the shelves to determine if it had simply been shelved wrong," Grizela continued, "but I couldn't find it anywhere."

"What book are you talking about?" Laura asked.

"*The Book of Poisons*, of course. You asked if Brendan Lancashire had borrowed it, and he hadn't. However, it's gone, so he could have taken it without signing it out." Grizela grimaced. "I mean, really. Stealing from the public library. What's next? Is nothing sacred anymore?" She scooped up her purse and the scone Laura offered her with a nod of thanks. "I need to get back and keep trying to find that book, or at least make sure no one steals any of the others."

"Anyone could have taken it," Molly said as the librarian disappeared through the bakehouse door.

"And a parking ticket for his mom's car is hardly enough to connect Brendan to the missing library book," Laura said.

"Certainly not enough for Officer Murdoch to secure a search warrant," Carol agreed.

"I wish I'd known about this yesterday," Laura said. "Henry paid Brendan a visit to encourage him to resume his schooling and equipment manager duties. I could have asked him to nose around for the book while he was there."

"I'm sure the boy wouldn't have it sitting out in plain view where his mom or sister would see it," Molly said.

"Unless one of them took it," Carol suggested. "Given the way the coach and team treat Brendan, I wouldn't be surprised if his family hadn't considered getting a little payback for him."

"Except that three of the first four incidents ended up putting more blame on him," Laura said. "Or, in the case of the poisoned water, it would have if he hadn't gotten sick first."

"Oh!" Molly exclaimed suddenly, pointing through the bakehouse's front window to a teen coming up the walk holding a wide box full of plants. "Our poinsettias are here."

"Before Thanksgiving?" Carol frowned. "It would have been nice if they'd waited another week or two. They don't exactly go with your autumn displays, Molly."

"It's no problem," Molly assured her. "I can store them in the office until we're ready to switch to Christmas decorations. They'll get plenty of sun in there." She went to the front door and let the young man inside. "No classes this morning?" she asked as she walked him to the counter and gestured for him to leave the flat there.

He shook his head as he set down his burden. "I have study hall this period, so I figured it was as good a time as any to start the team's deliveries."

"We appreciate your promptness." Molly bustled around the counter. "Let me get you a couple of biscuits as a thank-you."

"Thank you, ma'am," he said enthusiastically.

Molly quickly placed a few cookies in a paper bakery bag and handed it over. The lad thanked her again and left, and Carol and Laura went back to the kitchen.

A moment later, Molly entered, waving the order tag from the poinsettias. "Laura, wasn't there a Williams on our suspect list?"

"No, but the team's mascot is Kit Williams." Laura peered at her friend. "Why?"

Molly showed Laura the nursery tag. "These came from Williams Nursery. I was thinking they could have aloe vera plants too."

"And Brendan is friends with Kit," Carol put in.

Laura shook her head. "Do you really think Brendan would have drunk the water after poisoning it?"

"Maybe he just pretended to be sick," Molly said.

"He couldn't fake that green skin, and I heard enough to be convinced he wasn't putting on an act," Laura insisted, then nearly jolted at the memory of the previous day's visit to the Lancashire home. "Yesterday, Henry pointed out that Kit was wearing shoes that match the print found by Coach Bassett's car after the tires were deflated."

"Did you tell Murdoch?" Molly asked.

Laura groaned. "No. To be honest, I didn't want to get the boy in trouble. I figured if it was him, his heart was in the right place." She frowned at the nursery tag. "It didn't seem possible that he could be behind the other incidents."

"He might not be," Carol said. She pulled out her phone. "I'll text Bridget and ask if she checked the nursery for aloe. They might not even sell it." She sent the message and a moment later, the phone dinged with Bridget's reply. "She says they sell wholesale and hadn't had any recent orders for aloe vera."

"But they do carry it?" Molly clarified.

"Presumably," Carol said. "Should we call Murdoch?"

"Just because his family's nursery sells aloe vera, that doesn't mean Kit used it to poison the team's water canteen," Laura argued. "Why would he?"

"To avenge his friend, the same reason he deflated the coach's tires," Molly said.

Laura sighed as a memory floated back to her. "After the itching powder, I remember hearing Kit tell Brendan that at least the players would respect him because now they realized the power he wields being in control of their equipment."

"And when the team didn't start treating Brendan better, maybe Kit decided they needed another reminder," Carol speculated. "And that's why he sabotaged the equipment that failed when Henry was using it."

"I suppose it's possible," Laura conceded. "Henry did mention that Kit blamed the bus's busted gas line on bad karma. I assumed he was thinking of the way they tend to treat others, Brendan included. Maybe we're totally missing some other kid they like to pick on, someone no one notices."

"Why are you resisting the idea that it could be Kit?" Molly asked gently.

Laura shrugged. "I admire the way he stands up for the underdog. It saddens me to think he could be no better than the guys he has a problem with."

"You want to know the truth one way or the other, right?" Molly prodded.

"Yes." Laura removed her apron and glanced around the kitchen. "We're pretty well caught up here. Let me pay Mrs. Williams a visit." She copied the address from the plant tag into the map app on her phone. "It says it's fifteen minutes away, so I shouldn't be long."

Twenty minutes later, Laura steered into the driveway for Williams Nursery and groaned at the sight of the huge maple tree gracing the front lawn. This did not look good for Kit. Not only did he have avenging his friend as a motive, he clearly had means—an ample supply of maple keys to use to make itching powder, and no doubt an equally ample supply of aloe plants. Beyond that, he had opportunity, having been at every game and practice during which the incidents had occurred.

A petite woman with short dark hair emerged from a nearby greenhouse and approached the small parking area. "May I help you?" she asked as Laura climbed out of the Beetle.

"Are you Mrs. Williams?" Laura asked, though the woman's bright blue eyes and dimpled chin were the spitting image of Kit's.

"Yes. I'm sorry if you're here to buy stock for personal use. We sell wholesale."

"That's not why I'm here. I'm Laura Donovan, Henry Donovan's aunt." When Mrs. Williams didn't seem to know who he was, Laura added, "He's the football team's running back."

"Okay," Mrs. Williams said, still clearly confused.

"Are you Kit's mother?"

"That's right."

Laura nodded, scrambling for a subtle way to broach the subject, since none had occurred to her during the drive there. "You wouldn't have happened to notice any of your aloe vera plants missing, would you?"

The woman's head jerked with apparent surprise. "You found them?"

"Not exactly," Laura said. "So you are missing some?"

"Yes. I noticed this morning that I'm missing more than a dozen. I have no idea how long they've been gone. Kit has been watering in the greenhouses for me." The woman sighed. "I don't know what I'd do without him. His dad walked out on us last year, and I've been struggling to keep up with this place ever since. We took it over from my father-in-law, but my ex's heart was never in it. After he left, I expected him to demand it be sold and the value split, but he said I could keep it going for Kit to take over one day if he wanted it."

"That was decent of him," Laura murmured.

The woman snorted. "Except that he leveraged it as a way out of paying child support and alimony, so if we can't make it work, we don't eat."

Laura's heart hurt for the poor woman. "That certainly makes your offer of poinsettias at cost for the school fundraiser all the more generous."

The woman shrugged. "It was a way I could afford to help. Not so generous really. Anyway, you were asking about my missing aloe vera plants?"

Considering the woman's situation, Laura hated to suggest her son might be behind anything untoward. But if he was, he needed to be stopped. As her mother used to say: two wrongs don't make a right. Noticing a pile of plant debris a few yards away, Laura said, "Is that your compost pile?"

"Yes."

Laura eased closer to the pile and spotting the dried-out skin of an aloe leaf, reached down and picked it up. "When's the last time you composted any aloe plants?"

"I haven't." Mrs. Williams frowned as Laura showed her the leaf. "That's curious."

Laura scrutinized the pile more closely and toed at the area near where she'd spotted the leaf. Mrs. Williams retrieved a shovel from the greenhouse and quickly uncovered the remnants of probably a dozen decimated aloe plants.

"I don't believe this," she said, her voice unsteady. "They must have gotten diseased or something. Still, Kit knows better than to throw diseased plants on our compost pile. I can't believe he didn't mention them to me."

Laura picked up another of the leaves. Like the one she already held, it had been slit. Its dried-out appearance could be blamed on decomposition, but Laura suspected it had been stripped of its gel or at least the toxic substance surrounding it. She showed Mrs. Williams the evidence and gently conveyed her suspicions of Kit's involvement in the recent rash of incidents befalling the football team.

The woman chucked the telltale leaves back onto the compost pile. "It can't be Kit. He's a good boy."

"I feel the same way," Laura told her. "I've seen how he sticks up for kids who are mistreated. I'm afraid he might have taken his righteous indignation to the extreme, perhaps in a misguided attempt to either teach the bullies a lesson or to avenge their victims. Or both."

Mrs. Williams blinked back tears and sniffled. "That sounds like something Kit might do."

"Did you happen to notice a fuel stain on any of his clothes recently, or maybe automotive grease?"

"No. The only issue we've had lately with clothes was a tear in his mascot costume. Well, a piece ripped right out actually, so I couldn't just sew it back together. I had him take it to the dry cleaners for repair."

Laura's blood went cold. "Do you remember what color the torn fabric was?"

"Black."

The same color as the fabric she'd found by the sabotaged equipment. So, Kit was likely responsible for that mishap too. "Was Kit out at all Sunday night?" Laura asked.

Mrs. Williams thought for a moment. "I'm not sure where he was. I went to my mom's for the afternoon and ended up staying for supper. When I got home around nine, Kit was here doing homework. I didn't ask him if he'd been out."

No alibi then.

Struck by an urgent need to get to the high school before the football team's bus left for the tournament, Laura hurried toward her car. Noticing the maple tree once more, she stopped. "Have you seen Kit collecting maple keys, Mrs. Williams?"

"Always. He's been fascinated by them since he was a little boy. His dad showed him how they fly like helicopters."

Laura gave a solemn nod. "Forensics showed that the itching powder in the players' shoulder pads was made from maple keys."

Mrs. Williams gulped. "My brother pulled that prank on me when we were kids. I must have told Kit the story dozens of times."

"I'm sorry." Laura's heart ached for the woman at the additional damning piece of evidence against her son. However, a fresh wave of dread swamped her as she checked her watch and realized with great horror that the football team's bus was departing for their weekend tournament any moment.

And Kit, the misguided saboteur with a chip on his shoulder and a head full of creative ideas for making his enemies pay, would be on it.

20

Now convinced Kit had been their sole prankster, Laura drove to the school as quickly as she could. Surely the lad wouldn't do anything to jeopardize the team's chances at such a big tournament, she told herself, but she couldn't shake a sense of foreboding.

Laura's heart sank as she pulled into the school's half-empty parking lot and realized the bus was gone. She was too late.

Principal Groves flagged her down from the sidewalk.

She drove up beside him and lowered the window.

"Ms. Donovan, isn't it?" he asked, stooping to see her. "I'm afraid you've missed him. We let the bus leave early so there'd be no risk of their being late for the game." Mr. Groves pressed the button on his key fob and a beep sounded from a car two spaces away. "I'm heading there now myself if you want to follow me."

Laura sprang from her car. "Could I talk to you before you leave?" Her voice trembled but he didn't seem to notice.

"Can it wait until Monday? I'd hate to miss kickoff."

"No, it can't wait. I think I know who's behind all the pranks."

His eyes widened. She definitely had his attention. "Shall we go to my office?"

"No need." As much as Laura doubted Kit would sabotage today's game, for his school's sake, her urgency to get to the game was building by the second. She quickly shared her theory about Kit.

"I see." Principal Groves nodded solemnly, not seeming surprised by the revelation.

Her phone beeped a text message alert from Henry. Her eyes widened. "Moira and her cocaptain, Izzy, are missing," she reported to the principal. "Apparently, Moira drove to the game instead of taking the bus because she didn't want to be anywhere near the QB."

"Because of their breakup." Mr. Groves sighed. "The coach shouldn't have given her the option, but with everything that's been going on, a few parents chose to personally drive their kids to the game rather than have them take the bus."

Laura shook her head. "I don't like the sound of this. Kit was livid with Moira for humiliating Brendan. Brendan took it so hard that he stayed home from school and practice most of the week."

"Brendan was here this morning."

"That's because last night, Kit went to his house and assured him Moira had learned her lesson and wouldn't give him any more trouble. What if the reason Kit knew that was because he intended to ensure she never made it to the game?"

"You heard him say she learned her lesson?" Mr. Groves clarified.

"He told me himself. He said, 'I refreshed Moira's memory about what it feels like to be bullied. She won't be bothering him anymore.'" Laura shuddered. "I thought Kit meant he had reminded her of how her previous ex, Frank Aldridge, treated her after they broke up. But maybe Kit decided to give her a *fresh* taste of how it felt." Laura skimmed the latest text message from Henry. "Henry says none of the girls have been able to get Moira or Izzy on their cell phones."

"They could've had car trouble," Mr. Groves reasoned. "Moira drives a light blue Prius. I'll watch for it as I drive to the game." He handed Laura his business card. "Text me at this number if you receive any updates on their whereabouts."

"I will," Laura promised.

"Thank you for taking the time to report your suspicions. Rest assured we'll get to the bottom of this."

"I hope so," Laura replied. "I'll see you at the game."

She raced to her car and sped back to Bread on Arrival. "I need to leave for the game now," she announced the instant she rushed inside. "I'm afraid I can't wait until we close. Moira and her cocaptain are missing."

"Have you called Officer Murdoch?" Molly asked.

Laura blew out a breath. "No. I never thought to. I rushed over here as soon as I finished telling Mr. Groves about Kit." She gave them a condensed recap of the situation.

"You and Bridget go now," Carol ordered. "Molly and I will call Murdoch, then catch up with you at the game after we close the shop."

Bridget shed her apron and grabbed her hat, coat, and bag. "I'm ready."

Molly filled two cups with coffee and bagged a few pastries. "For the road," she said, handing it to Laura.

"Thanks," Laura said. "Pray Kit hasn't done something really stupid."

Once in the car, Laura typed the address of the game into her phone's GPS. "Watch for a light-blue Prius," she told Bridget.

"Got it." Bridget scanned their surroundings as they drove. After a few minutes, she asked, "Do you think Kit did something to Moira's car?"

"Honestly, I don't know what to think."

Police lights flashed in her rearview mirror, growing closer. Laura eased her foot off the accelerator and pulled to the side of the road. A moment later, the cruiser sped past them.

"That was a Loch Mallaig cruiser," Bridget said.

"Really?" Laura resumed her previous speed. "Maybe it was Murdoch. Call Henry and ask if anything's happened."

"You got it." Bridget dialed Henry and put her phone on speaker. When he answered, she explained about the cruiser and asked if there was trouble.

"No, and Moira's absence was a false alarm," Henry said. "She and Izzy showed up. I texted Aunt Laura, but I must have forgotten to hit *send*. The message is still in my drafts."

The tension eased from Laura's shoulders. "That's a relief. We'll be there soon." Bridget ended the call and Laura said, "How annoyed do you think Murdoch will be about being summoned to the game for nothing?"

Bridget waved off Laura's concern. "He'll probably be happy for the excuse to attend." She flashed Laura a crooked smile. "Can't say the same for when he finds out you solved his case without him."

"Let's just hope Kit doesn't have another prank planned, or Murdoch might get the chance to play the hero yet."

A short while later, they arrived at the host school's football field. The parking lot was full, so Laura snagged a spot on the street. She and Bridget walked to the stadium, and an unwelcome sight greeted them around the side of the bleachers. Larry the Loon was dancing in front of the stands, flapping his wings to rally the fans.

"I guess Mr. Groves decided not to punish Kit by pulling him from his mascot duties," Laura said, disappointed.

As if on cue, the principal materialized at her side. "I told Kit we'd talk after the game and to watch his step."

Curious how readily Kit would admit to everything, Laura asked, "Did he give the impression he knew what this talk was concerning?"

"Not in the least." Mr. Groves frowned. "And with all my years dealing with students, I can usually get an accurate read on them. He may not be our man."

"Or he doesn't show any signs of guilt because he doesn't think what he did was wrong," Bridget suggested.

"I can count on one hand the number of students I've had over the years who were almost devoid of a conscience," the principal replied. "Kit Williams is *not* one of them. He's one of the most moral kids I know."

"That's my point," Bridget said. "He might be blinded by the belief that the victims got what they deserved."

"I said as much to Kit's mom," Laura said, "and she agreed it sounded like the way he might think."

"Well, not to worry." Groves flapped a hand. "Now that he knows I'm watching him, I'm sure he won't get up to any more nonsense."

As Laura and Bridget approached Henry to wish him luck in the game, cheerleading cocaptain Izzy raced out to the coach along with a couple of other cheerleaders. "We can't find Moira," Izzy blurted.

"I thought she drove here with you," Bassett said.

"She did," Izzy said. "We were getting ready, but then she stepped out of the locker room to take a call because the reception was lousy. And now we can't find her. No one's seen her."

"I'm sure she'll turn up," Bassett said impatiently. "I can't worry about it now. The game is about to begin. If she doesn't show up, you'll have to do without her."

Laura exchanged a glance with Bridget, silently agreeing that they needed to chat with Kit. Laura hugged Henry and wished him luck, then she and Bridget hurried toward Larry the Loon, entertaining fans in the stands.

Officer Murdoch must have realized something was up because he intercepted them on the way. "What's going on?"

They filled him in on everything, most of which he'd already heard from Principal Groves, then he strode with them toward Kit.

When they were still several yards away, the officer called, "Kit, can we have a word?"

The boy took off in the opposite direction.

Laura and Murdoch chased after him while Bridget cut through the grandstands to try to head him off.

"I clearly need to stop neglecting my running routine," Laura muttered as she struggled to close the distance. The teen was surprisingly fast for someone weighed down by ten pounds of feathers.

With a firm swing of her tote, Bridget halted Kit's flight a few yards past the stands. Murdoch passed Laura and hurled himself at their stunned feathered friend, tackling him to the ground. Fortunately, the football teams chose that moment to jog onto the field, drawing everyone's attention to the game instead of the kerfuffle.

Murdoch hauled Kit to his feet and dragged off the boy's head cover. Laura sucked in a sharp breath. "You're not Kit."

21

"Where's Kit? What did you do to him?" Bridget demanded of the scrawny, unfamiliar teen still struggling for breath after his flight.

"I haven't done anything to him," the lad squeaked.

"Then why did you run?" Murdoch asked.

"Because I thought I'd be in trouble for filling in for Kit."

"Where is he?" Laura asked.

The boy waved his feathered arm. "Around here somewhere. He wanted some time to hang with his girl."

"His girl?" Laura was pretty sure Moira wouldn't appreciate the moniker. "Did you see this girl?"

"No," the teen said. "I didn't even know he had a girlfriend until today. Is he in some kind of trouble? I'm supposed to meet him in the locker room after the first quarter so he can get back into costume."

"You'd better get back out there and lead our fans," Murdoch told the kid. "Then keep your rendezvous with Kit."

The lad nodded and donned the loon head once more.

"Don't tell Kit about our conversation," the officer warned.

"Okay." The boy's voice wobbled, and Laura was pretty sure his nervousness alone would give away to Kit that he'd been found out—if they didn't find him first.

"Do we wait until the end of first period and ambush him?" Bridget asked as the imposter headed back to his post.

"That'll be too late." Laura scanned the perimeter of the field.

"Whatever he plans to do, he expects to have it finished by then."

"And he expects the fact that his imposter is in full view of the fans the whole time will give him an alibi," Murdoch concluded.

"Did you see that?" Bridget pointed to a copse of pines beyond the far end of the field. "I saw a flash of the school's colors. Maybe it was Moira's cheerleading outfit."

Murdoch pointed. "You two go that way around the field. I'll go the other way to head off anyone who tries to run."

Laura reached the trees first. At the sound of rustling, she signaled Bridget to follow her lead. Taking advantage of the cover provided by a large evergreen, Laura scanned the area. A tripod with a cell phone attached stood in the center of a clearing enclosed by the circle of trees. She followed the aim of the lens and gasped when she saw a gagged Moira bound to a tree.

Laura sprinted across the clearing to Moira and removed the gag. "Are you okay?"

"Thank goodness you found me," the girl gasped as Bridget started on the ropes around the girl's legs.

"Who did this to you?" Laura asked, working on the knots digging into her wrists.

"Turn off the camera," Moira told Bridget as Officer Murdoch appeared from the other direction.

The officer examined the tripod. "It's not on."

"It's not?" The girl seemed to crumple with relief. "He said he was livestreaming me to the school's social media so I'd know what it felt like to be humiliated the way Izzy and I humiliated Brendan." Tears streamed down her cheeks. "I didn't mean to. I didn't realize how awful we were to him. I thought the whole thing was a joke, honest. I felt bad when he confronted me about it. I honestly did. But then when Izzy made a joke about Brendan outside the locker room today, I couldn't help laughing. He heard me. Said he thought I'd learned my lesson."

"Who said? Who did this to you?" Officer Murdoch asked.

Moira massaged her newly released wrists. "It doesn't matter. I kind of deserved it. When he first left me here, I was so angry, but then I was scared and alone and afraid no one would ever find me. Then I got freaked out by thoughts of how the kids at school would laugh over the whole thing when they saw it online. And then I realized that's how guys like Brendan must feel a lot." She studied the ground, clearly ashamed.

Officer Murdoch examined the phone. "Is this Kit's?"

"No, it's mine," Moira answered. She told him the password so he could unlock the screen.

"It wasn't livestreaming," he reported a moment later. "And it doesn't appear that any photos or videos were taken."

"Do you feel up to cheering with your squad?" Laura asked. "You have a lot of friends worried about you."

Moira swiped at her damp cheeks. "Could I go to the restroom to freshen up first?"

"Of course." Laura offered her an arm to lean on.

Murdoch handed Moira her cell phone, then collapsed the tripod and tucked it under his arm. "I need to know who did this to you so I can press charges for forcible confinement."

Moira shook her head. "I don't want to press charges."

"What he did was wrong," the officer said.

"We all did a lot of things wrong," Moira said. "I see that now. I can't say I'm happy about what he did, but I understand why he did it."

"We know Kit was behind the other pranks," Laura said gently as she walked Moira back to the school. "As noble as his intentions might've been, what he did was still wrong, and he needs to be held accountable."

"I don't know anything about the other stuff," Moira said. As they approached the school door, she freed her arm from the crook of Laura's. "Thank you for finding me."

"The first quarter is almost over," Murdoch said after Moira went inside. "I guess I'll wait in the locker room for Kit."

"No need," Laura said. "Here he comes now."

Kit's gaze collided with theirs and his pace slowed, but he didn't run. "Hey, Ms. D. How's it going?"

"Good." Laura smiled and hoped it didn't look as fake as it felt.

"Why aren't you in costume?" Murdoch asked.

"Stewart's always wanted a chance to play mascot, so I said he could have a go during the first quarter. I'm meeting him now to switch over."

"He said you wanted time to hang with your girlfriend," Bridget said. "Where is she?"

Kit chuckled. "I said that so he would think he was doing me a favor instead of the other way around." He shrugged as if being so noble came naturally. He didn't seem the least bit fazed by their questioning.

Could they be wrong in assuming he was the one who had trussed Moira to the tree? She hadn't actually named him. They had no proof it was him at all—unless Murdoch dusted the tripod for prints. Laura glanced at Kit's hands. He was wearing gloves.

"So, what have you been doing this whole time, Kit?" Murdoch asked.

The boy shrugged. "Watching the game."

Mr. Groves approached from the direction of the field. "Kit? If you're here, who's that?" He pointed to Larry the Loon.

"It's Stewart, sir," Kit said politely. "He's always wanted a chance to play our mascot and I didn't see the harm. I'll go resume my mascot duties."

Murdoch caught him by the back of the collar. "Not so fast. I'm not finished with you."

Kit didn't fight the officer's hold, but he stared beseechingly at the principal. "I know I shouldn't have let Stewart do it without permission, but is it really necessary to involve the police?"

Laura frowned. *Oh, he is a cool cucumber.*

Mr. Groves raised an eyebrow at Murdoch. "Is there something else going on I should know about?"

"We believe Kit kidnapped your head cheerleader and confined her against her will."

The color drained from Kit's face as Groves grew alarmed. "Moira is missing?"

Moira chose that moment to step out of the locker room. She waved as she scurried past them toward the field.

"As you can see, she's not missing now, sir," the officer said. "We found her tied up in the trees over there, but she refused to identify the person responsible."

"That's not exactly true," Laura said, thinking she might know how to wheedle a confession out of Kit after all. "She did mention Brendan." Laura turned to Bridget. "Maybe you could run and ask Brendan to join us."

Bridget hurried off and was back a moment later with Brendan. The equipment manager glanced from Kit to the loon mascot in obvious confusion. "What's going on?"

"That's what we'd like to know," Officer Murdoch said, apparently catching on to Laura's strategy. "You do realize forcible confinement is an indictable offense, don't you?"

"Forcible what?" Brendan appeared so stunned that Laura immediately regretted the tactic. "What are you talking about?"

To his credit, Kit immediately spoke up. "Brendan didn't do anything."

"And how do you know that?" Murdoch asked.

Kit ducked his head. "Because I pulled the pranks."

"You?" Brendan choked out.

"Those guys are always picking on you," Kit argued. "They're always picking on anyone who can't throw a football, or who doesn't look good in a cheerleading outfit, or who is smarter than them. They needed to be brought down a peg, to realize they can't power trip by trampling on the rest of us."

"Coach thought it was me," Brendan countered.

A muscle in Kit's cheek flinched. "I didn't mean for that to happen."

"My nephew could have been seriously injured by your actions," Laura put in. "And he's never bullied anyone, has he?"

Kit stiffened. "Maybe not, but he doesn't stop it either. He condones it by his silence."

Laura gaped at him. "You don't see it, do you?"

Kit crossed his arms. "See what?"

"You're as guilty of bullying as they are," she said.

"They were never going to get how it felt until it happened to them," Kit reasoned. "They needed to be taught a lesson."

"It doesn't matter that you're targeting bullies with your bullying tactics. It's still wrong." Laura shook her head. "You know what, I sincerely admired you for the way you stood up to the guys who picked on Brendan and for confronting Frank for picking on Moira, and even for confronting Moira for picking on Brendan—the first time. It takes a strong character to stand up for what's right, alone against the mob. It's unfortunate, however, that you felt the need to stoop to their level to get back at them. And you hurt other people in the process."

Coach Bassett strode up to their growing group. "Brendan! Where's the water?" The coach's gaze skipped from Murdoch to Mr. Groves to Laura. "What's going on here?"

"We caught your prankster," Murdoch informed him.

Bassett's eyes flared at Kit. "You?"

"You deserved it," Kit spat. "You're as bad as your players."

"Your actions could have cost some of those boys college scholarships if we hadn't managed to win anyway," the coach growled, an angry flush creeping up his neck.

Kit snorted derisively. "See? All you care about is winning. Meanwhile, you treat people like Brendan like garbage."

"Okay, that's enough." Mr. Groves dismissed Bassett with a brisk nod, then informed Kit he would be stripped of his mascot duties permanently and suspended for what he'd done. "I'll drive you home, Kit," the principal finished. "Your mother might like to know what you've been up to."

"But what about the football players and cheerleaders?" Bridget interjected. "They should be held accountable for their actions too, don't you think? I mean, making classmates emotionally ill by belittling them is no better than making them sick to their stomachs. In fact, I'd say it's worse because it lingers and festers."

"She's got a point," Laura said.

"You're right, of course," Mr. Groves said. "Trust me, I will address that too, but now is not the time."

Realizing there was nothing else they could do at the moment, Laura and Bridget went back to the stands just as Molly and Carol arrived with Beth Templeton.

"We told her she could come," Carol explained, then pointed to the cheerleaders. "I see they found Moira."

Laura and Bridget gave a quick recounting of recent events with promises to go into more detail later when they were in a more private setting.

"You figured out Kit was behind everything?" Beth asked Laura. Her face crumpled. "There's no way Dalziel will want to date me now."

"Why on earth would you say that?" Laura asked.

"I'll be a constant reminder of his ineptitude as an investigator," Beth answered, her face stricken.

The officer in question appeared a few yards behind Beth, and Laura wondered how much he'd heard. She cringed and gestured for Beth to stop talking, but the substitute teacher paid her no mind.

"I so wanted to be the one to help him find his wings," Beth went on as Murdoch came closer. "Dalziel's smart, you know. You might not realize it because he lacks a bit of confidence, but he doesn't miss much. The confidence will come with more experience."

The young officer cleared his throat, his cheeks pink.

With a gasp, Beth spun around. "Dalziel," she choked out. "I didn't see you there."

"Hi, Beth." Murdoch smiled shyly. He jerked a thumb at the bleachers. "Would you like to watch the game together?"

A besotted expression transformed Beth's features, and she beamed as she slipped her hand around his offered elbow. The pair went off and found seats on their own, and once they were out of earshot, the Bakehouse Three erupted into a fit of giggles.

The ache in Laura's heart started to lessen. At least something good had come out of all the drama of the past few weeks.

The Monday afternoon following the semifinals, Laura helped collect leftover baked goods from the bakehouse's display cases at closing. "I thought we'd be busier so close to Thanksgiving."

"I suspect everyone is still tired after the big weekend," Molly said, smiling. "Celebrating our Loch Mallaig Loons winning the state tournament is a once-in-a-lifetime opportunity."

"Hopefully not." Hamish swiped a cloth across the table he'd cleared. "I fully expect to have a similar celebration next fall." He grabbed the newspaper that had been on the table and brought it to Laura. "Would you like to keep this?"

"Yes, please." Laura accepted the paper and felt a fresh thrill at the sight of the photo on the front page that showed the Loons rushing the football field after Henry's game-winning touchdown. A beaming Brendan was being carried on the players' shoulders, supported by the team he'd supported all season long through thick and thin.

Carol paused in counting the cash in the till. "Laura, I forgot to tell you that Grizela stopped in today. She thought you'd like to know that Mrs. Williams returned *The Book of Poisons* to the library. She found it under Kit's mattress. Apparently he'd borrowed Brendan's car for a day or two while his was in the shop. Since the car is in Brendan's mother's name, the ticket was issued to her when Kit parked it in front of the fire hydrant at the library."

"Interesting," Laura said. Thinking about another unanswered question, she said, "I never heard what happened with the bus's gas line, though. Did any of you?"

"That actually wasn't Kit." Henry emerged from the back hallway and dropped his backpack on one of the chairs. Although his parents had returned to the States in time for the big game, he hadn't transferred schools yet—and he didn't seem to be in any hurry to, either. "The driver finally admitted that he'd been checking his phone and drove over a downed tree limb on his way to the high school to pick up the boys. It ripped the gas line, but he knew he'd get in trouble for being on his phone if he told the truth."

"I certainly hope he's held accountable," Carol said. "Imagine if that tree limb had damaged the brake line instead. He could have really hurt someone."

"Speaking of accountability, is the principal doing anything to discipline the coach and players for their bullying?" Molly asked Henry.

"All the school teams are taking an anti-bullying seminar, including the coaches," Henry said. "I feel like I've seen some changes around school already." He gestured toward the newspaper Laura held.

"Glad to hear it," Laura said.

"We also have to give all our poinsettia fundraiser money to the track team for their pole-vaulting equipment," Henry reported. "The guys are annoyed, but I'm really happy Amy's going to have the gear she needs to do well this year."

"That's very big of you," Carol said. "Officer Murdoch was in earlier. He mentioned that when he dropped Kit off Saturday, Mrs. Williams already had the perfect reparation in mind for him. She plans to have him grow 500 flats of spring bedding plants to donate for a similar spring fundraiser."

"That should keep him out of trouble," Molly said.

Brightening, Henry grinned. "All of that is great, but it's not what I rushed over here to tell you, Aunt Laura," he said, practically bouncing on his toes. "The recruiter from the University of South Carolina contacted me."

Laura's heart tripped over a beat. "What did he say?"

Henry beamed. "They want to recruit me."

"That's incredible news!" Laura rushed forward and hugged her nephew, knowing she couldn't be prouder of him if he were her own son. When she drew back, she gestured to the snowflakes gently swirling outside the window. "South Carolina is a good place to get away from the snow."

"It sure is," Henry agreed. "But you know I'll come back and visit whenever I can."

"And you'll be welcome anytime." Laura pulled him in for another hug, knowing that no matter where he went, her nephew would always have a place in her home and her heart, just as she had found her place in Loch Mallaig.

Up to this point, we've been doing all the writing. Now it's *your* turn!

Tell us what you think about this book, the characters, the bad guy, or anything else you'd like to share with us about this series. We can't wait to hear from *you*!

Log on to give us your feedback at:
https://www.surveymonkey.com/r/ScottishBakehouse

Annie's® FICTION